FIC 35/23
DW

E 2

ABOUT THE AUTHOR

KATHRYN HARRISON is the author of the novels *The Binding Chair, Poison, Exposure,* and *Thicker Than Water.* She has also written a memoir, *The Kiss.* Her personal essays have appeared in *The New Yorker, Harper's Magazine,* and other publications. She lives in New York with her husband, the novelist Colin Harrison, and their children. She can be reached at thebindingchair@yahoo.com.

Also by Kathryn Harrison

THE BINDING CHAIR

THE KISS

POISON

EXPOSURE

THICKER THAN WATER

THE SEAL WIFE

THE SEAL WIFE

A NOVEL

Kathryn Harrison

RANDOM HOUSE

NEW YORK

First published in Great Britain in 2002 by
Fourth Estate
A Division of HarperCollins *Publishers*
77–85 Fulham Palace Road,
London W6 8JB
www.4thestate.com

Book design by Casey Hampton

Printed in great Britain by
Clays Ltd, St Ives plc

H.S.J.

1890–1984

THE SEAL WIFE

HE IS TWENTY-SIX, and for as long as he's lived in the north there has been only the Aleut woman.

Several evenings a week he comes to her door with a duck or a rabbit and she asks him in. Not asks, exactly. She opens the door and steps aside so he can enter.

She lives in a frame house hammered together fast out of boards and tar paper, a house like all the others in Anchorage, except it isn't on First or Fourth or even Ninth Street; instead it is off to the east, marooned on the mud flats. But she has things in it, like anyone else, a table and two chairs, flour and tea on a shelf, a hat hanging from a peg. She wears a dress with buttons and she cooks at a stove, and the two of them eat before, and then after she sits cross-legged in the tub and smokes her pipe.

She smokes, and he watches her smoke. He thinks her mouth may be the most beautiful part of her—not red, not brown or mauve or pink, but a color for which he has no name. Her top lip is finely drawn, almost stern; the bottom one is plump, with a crease in the center. On another face its fullness might be considered a pout, but her black eyes convey none of the disappointment, nor the invitation, of such an expression.

She is the only woman who has allowed him to watch her as intently, as much and as long, as he wants, and the reason for this comes to him one night. She is self-possessed. There is nothing he can take from her by looking.

At the thought, he gets up from the bed and goes to the window, he rests his forehead on its cold pane. She possesses herself. How much more this makes him want her!

Then, one day, it's over: she won't open her door to him.

He knocks, he rattles the knob. "Please," he says, his mouth against the crack. "Open up. It's me."

With his hands cupped around his eyes, he peers through the window and there she is, sitting at the table, staring at the wall.

He knocks on the glass and holds up his rabbit, but she doesn't turn her head. Even after he's walked the entire perimeter of the two-room house, hitting the boards with the heel of his hand, even after that, when he looks in the window, he sees her still sitting there, not moving. He leaves his dead rabbit on the ground and goes back the way he came, trudging past the railroad yard and the new bunkhouse, the sawmill with its chained curs lunging and snapping after his shadow.

What. He thinks the word over and over. There must be some explanation. But what?

It's June, eleven o'clock at night and bright as morning. The usually gray water of the inlet is purple, gold where the light touches it, a low skein of cirrus unraveling on the horizon. Beyond the trampled mud of the streets are wildflowers growing everywhere, flowers of all colors, red fireweed, yellow broom, blue aster. He picks them as he walks. Preoccupied, he yanks at them, and some come up roots and all. After smelling their bright heads, he drops them, and by the time he retraces his path their petals have withered.

Has he done something to offend her? In his mind he reviews his last visit with the woman. He brought her a duck, a good-size one, and a bolt of netting to protect her bed. Surely there was nothing wrong in that. He can't stand being bitten by mosquitoes, and he hates for the two of them to have to leave their clothing on. Every hour he's not with her is one spent waiting to see her, the more of her the better. She has the sloping shoulders characteristic of her people; breasts that are small and pointed, like two halves of a yam set side by side; three black lines tattooed on her chin; and smooth, bowed legs.

She, he calls her to himself, because he hasn't presumed to name her, not even privately. Her hair is long and black, a mare's tail, and once, when he began to unbraid it, she took it from his hands. By some accident of biology her navel turned out a perfect spiral, and he's fought off her hands to kiss her in that place.

Her body seems young to him, as young as his own, as strong and unmarked. But her eyes make him wonder.

There's no point in asking her age, because she doesn't understand English, nor any of the pidgin phrases he's taught himself and tried to say.

Or perhaps she does know the meaning of his words but is unwilling to betray her knowledge—herself—to him.

Whether she understood him or not, the woman's silence did not stop him from talking; it provoked him, and he spoke more volubly to her than he had to anyone else, more than he might to a person who answered. His father was dead, he told her, and his mother and sister ran a boardinghouse in St. Louis. He'd lived in three cities so far: St. Louis, where he was born; Chicago, where he attended the university and earned a degree in mathematics; and Seattle, where he worked for two years as an observer for the Weather Bureau. Well, Seattle wasn't much of a city, he guessed, shaking his head. But compared to Anchorage.

When he talked she stopped what she was doing and watched him, and sometimes he could see himself, reflected on the wet surface of her eyes, and forgot what he had been saying. Oh, yes, he'd come north for the government land auction and he'd built the weather station from the same green lumber from which her house was made. But while she had only one window, he had windows all around. If she'd come outside with him, come with him to his station house, she'd see that the panes were six feet wide and as thick as this. To illustrate, he held his thumb and forefinger an inch apart.

But the woman, who allowed him to enter whenever he pleased, would not follow him so much as a foot beyond her door, and so they never walked together, never even stepped outside to watch the birds fly overhead.

Because it is his vocation, he often spoke to her of weather and its measurement. He is building a kite, a box kite as big as her bedroom, and to show her he paced off its dimensions. It will go up for miles and tell him what he can't determine from instruments on the ground.

There are tornadoes in Missouri, he told her, his finger stirring the air before her face, and he told her that as a child he walked through fields sown with shards of his grandmother's plates. A storm took and emptied her cupboards, carried off spoons and bowls and jars of peaches, and spun them over rivers and across roads, clear into the next county. "What do you think of that?" he said.

In Alaska, he'd traveled as far north as Talkeetna; he went with a trapper who accepted ten silver dollars to serve as his guide. The journey inland took three weeks, but coming back the wind picked up, and the trapper stuck a sail on his sled. They whistled down the frozen river, his ears singing with cold inside his parka hood, and he tried to keep his eyes open, because what he saw was not like anything he'd seen before: pink snow and blue forest, the kind of thing you expect in a dream but not while awake.

"Bigelow," he said, pointing to himself, clapping his hand on his chest, but he couldn't get her to repeat his name.

"Promise me something," he said. They were sitting side by side on her bed, dressed only in their boots, and when he stroked her knee, she looked down at his hand. In his mind, Bigelow ran through women—girls—he'd known. Karen, to whom he'd written a letter each day; Molly, very pretty, often looking past him to find her own reflection; Rachel, too tall, but it hadn't really mattered; Anne, reading a novel. They seemed even farther from him than the cities where they lived, and it was the attempt to conjure their faces that measured this distance. How tiny they were, like well-wishers waving from a shrinking dock.

Five days to sail north from Seattle. Bigelow disembarked in Anchorage, and by the time he'd thought to turn himself around and look back toward the ship that had brought him, it was gone. Anchorage—a place for ships to pause, to drop anchor for only as long as it might take to disgorge freight and passengers. To fill their holds with otter, mink, and sable, skins so fresh they still bled, packed in salt to keep them from spoiling.

"Promise me there's no one else."

This time he whispered the words, and the woman looked at him. She frowned and she put her fingers to her lips. The knuckles were so smooth, so sleek, that he wondered if northern people weren't, like the animals, insulated against the cold by a layer of yellow, silky fat.

.   .   .

October November December. January February March. April May. Half of June. Long enough for him to begin to take it for granted: he would knock, she would open.

Whatever else occupies him, Bigelow's thoughts return to the Aleut woman. He imagines their reunion, his passionate reentry into her house, into her arms, her body. But these fantasies don't get as far as the bed, the bed piled with skins. They're interrupted by the picture he has of her, sitting, staring, her hands folded in her lap, her thick black braid hanging over one shoulder.

Panicked—what's to become of him, what will he do? what will he do if she continues to refuse to see him?—he forces himself to let a day pass, and then another. He makes himself wait for what seems to him a long time, enough time for a woman to recover from whatever has upset her. Then he returns to her door.

But he finds it unlocked and inside her house nothing, just a pale spot on the floorboards where her bed used to be, and another under the missing stove. In one corner is his gramophone and, stacked neatly in their glassine envelopes, the Caruso and Tetrazzini recordings that he cranked the handle to play for her.

He walks around her two rooms. He runs his fingers along the walls until he comes to the place where she tacked up an illustrated advertisement for corsets, the fourteen styles available from the American Corset Company in Dayton, Ohio. Why she put it up or what she thought of it he cannot guess.

He stares at the advertisement, touches it, mouthing the names of the styles—Delineator, Posture Fix, Widow-Maker. He turns and with his back against the wall, he slides down, staring from one empty room into the other. He starts to cry, stops himself when he hears the choked noise he is making in the silence of her house. So small, so inadequate for the grief he feels.

PART ONE

JULY 10, 1915. He arrives in Anchorage without so much as a heavy coat or felt boot liners. Without matches, knife, or snow glasses. Having never held a gun. Sent north by the government, he makes the mistake of assuming he is going somewhere instead of nowhere: a field of mud under flapping canvas tents, two thousand railroad workers and no place to put them, a handful of women, and hour-long lines to buy dinner or a loaf of bread. A vast cloud of tiny, biting flies has settled in like fog, and mosquitoes swarm in predatory black columns. After a week he doesn't itch anymore, but his skin feels thick, and the mirror in his shaving kit shows an unfamiliar face, cheeks puffed up red and hard and eyes narrow like a native's. "Bigelow," he says, to hear his own name. Silently, he tells the red face not to worry. Not to worry so much. Who doesn't feel disoriented when he moves to a new place?

The surveyors who come north for the land auction look at the official blueprint he carries with him, stamped in one corner by the Weather Bureau, and then roll it back up and drop it in its tube. They give him a parcel of land by the creek and some advice on how best to spend his meager building allowance.

"Hire Indians," they say. "And don't pay them in liquor."

So he uses a crew of Chugach to knock together the two-story station, a square room on the ground for bed and stove and table, and above it a square observation room outfitted with windows on all sides. Getting the carpenters is easy. For a fee, an agent negotiates the wage and the length of a workday. Directing the five men is another matter.

Given to understand, both by the Weather Bureau and by friends in Seattle with experience in Alaska, that Chinook is the lingua franca of the north, Bigelow owns a pocket dictionary of the jargon. Including translations of the Ten Commandments, the Lord's Prayer, and the Pledge of Allegiance, it is no more than a booklet, and he memorized the few hundred equivalents on board ship as he sailed toward his new home, expecting to make himself understood by Indians, as well as by Russians and Swedes, anyone he might encounter there. But either he speaks it incorrectly—mispronouncing the words, stringing them in the wrong order—or the Chugach pretend ignorance.

"*T'zum pe-pah tum-tum.*" Bigelow shows them the government station plan. *Picture idea* is what he's said, the closest he can get to *blueprint,* a drawing he wants them to follow.

The men don't answer, they don't nod. Instead, they laugh, as if they've never seen anything as funny as the weather observatory he intends for them to assemble from the piles of lumber he's bought from the mill.

The only way he gets them to settle down to the job is by playing Caruso recordings, a tactic he discovers by chance when he unpacks and cranks his gramophone, just to see: does it still work? Yes, the tenor's brazenly rich voice pours from the horn with effortless splendor, and all five of the Chugach sit down on the ground in shock, as if an especially potent and invisible medicine man has announced his presence. Placed on the flat rock Bigelow uses for table and desk, the black box of the gramophone shivers as it plays. One of the crew—the strongest, whose face has the bland and amiable quality of a prize steer—crawls under Bigelow's tent flaps and refuses to come back out, not even after the gramophone's needle has been lifted. When his brother at last coaxes him into the light, he makes a wide and terrified berth around the bewitched mechanism and runs back toward the town site. On subsequent mornings, all Bigelow has to do is slip the black disc from its envelope, and the remaining crew jumps to attention and begins hammering.

Grateful for his accidental success, Bigelow still finds something awful in it. Perhaps what he fears is true: he's arrived in a land that will insist on its strangeness, where not only a dictionary but everything he's taught himself will prove useless.

Blueprint discarded, Bigelow relies on explanatory charades, which work well enough—the men follow his gestures—but it doesn't matter that he won't pay them with alcohol. His carpenters spend their wages as they want; and while they arrive each morning ready to work, on time and seemingly sober, as the weeks wear on, the station they build gets drunker and drunker. Not a beam is level, nor a corner square, and the staircase, especially besotted, collapses before the top floor is finished. Lacking proper stringers, it falls down in the middle of one windy night, stricken timber groaning before the treads begin their precipitous descent. Awakened in his tent, Bigelow lights a kerosene lamp and carries it outside and through the open door. He is looking for a foraging bear—the only explanation he has conceived for the noise. But the station is empty, the stairs have fallen under the weight of their own instability, and Bigelow holds up the lamp to watch as shrouds of golden sawdust blow over their remains.

The next day, he fires his crew and they depart hastily, their termination having been accomplished by back-to-back performances of Verdi and Leoncavallo. It's another month before Bigelow reassembles the stairs, the project slowed by a shortage of nails that plagues the entire settlement. Two crates of them are to arrive on the same ship that brings Bigelow's windowpanes, but once unpacked, both boxes are discovered filled with misaddressed nutmeg graters—useless in a place without even one imported kernel of the spice; the Chugach buy the graters cheap and sew them to their dance rattles, and the nails that hold the crates together (along with nails salvaged from every other packing box on board) sell for ten cents apiece, nine cents more than Bigelow can afford.

But the conditions under which the territory's official meteorologist sleeps and eats and works make no difference to the weather. Bigelow's anemometer turns and clicks in the wind; his ground thermometers are sunk into the earth to the official standardized depths of 30, 60, and 120 centimeters; his copper siphon rain recorder, complete with tipping bucket and weekly float gauges, bolted to its thirty-centimeter platform. He has adjusted his aneroid barometer to reflect his position at forty feet above sea level, and housed it along with the wet and dry bulb atmospheric thermometers in the louvered shed he assembled upon arrival. His snow measurement apparatus—density tube and spring balance, as well as a Kadel snow stake—is poised for the first flake's arrival.

Each morning he goes to the telegraph office, walking on boards laid over the mud. There he cables his observations on the weather to Washington, D.C., where bureau clerks and cartographers plot temperatures and pressures, precipitation indexes and wind speeds, from all over the country onto composite maps that reveal the direction and severity of storms, the arrival of killing frosts, the patterns of drought. Because of the earth's rotation, winter storms that paralyze the east originate in the west, and Bigelow's eight A.M. report will provide the Weather Bureau its earliest warning of trouble to come, as much as another day, or night, for farmers to thresh and for ranchers to gather their livestock into barns, for Great Lakes passenger boats to quickly find a port, for orange growers in Okeechobee County, Florida, to light smudge pots among their trees.

Bulletins. Warnings. Advisories. The Weather Bureau was once a division of the Army Signal Corps and speaks the language of alarm. Famous for its mercilessly swift transfers, for personnel orders effective within forty-eight hours, the bureau gave Bigelow just that long to book his passage and pack what he owned—no time to worry about where he was going until he was standing on the deck of the *Siren* as it left Seattle, his sudden apprehension almost something he could see, a lead-blue haze hanging over him, burnt off in spots by the hilarity of other passengers, fortune seekers from San Francisco and Portland and even New York, Chinese packed into steerage like consignments of firecrackers, a flock of Tanaina women returning from a year's employment in Vancouver.

Not exactly seasick, Bigelow stood on the *Siren*'s quarterdeck, looking backward at the wake, trying to imagine what he'd hurriedly read about Cook Inlet: one of the greatest tidal differentials in the world, chunks of ice as big as houses, as big as courthouses, ebbing and flowing as much as sixty miles in half a day. All the epic white buildings he'd seen: St. Louis's Festival Hall and her Palace of Horticulture. Chicago's Art Institute. Supreme courts and municipal courts. Legislatures. Opera houses. Departments of Commerce and Agriculture. The Weather Bureau and even the White House itself, dome cracking and colonnade collapsing. Having lost sight of land, Bigelow saw all of civilization's big white edifices turning and jumbling on great curling spits of freezing foam.

The fantasy of a city boy, he shrugged it off and went below deck, sat on his narrow bunk, and stared at the wall. For another eight dollars he could have had a porthole, he could have had the sky.

Except that it isn't a fantasy; it turns out to be true. In October, ice appears. With his binoculars, Bigelow watches the last ships of the season stalk and catch great slabs of it, haul them up in nets, pack them in sawdust, and return south to San Francisco's restaurants and butchers, to the ice cream parlors on Clay Street.

And in October, Bigelow receives an unofficial letter from a friend in the bureau, who warns that the department's new budget hasn't been approved, with salaries for Bigelow's rank stuck at the impossible $1,100 per year. How is he faring in Anchorage? the friend inquires. Does a town so new have a pool hall or a dance pavilion or moving-picture shows? Is there any opportunity for social gathering, female company?

Bigelow crumples the letter and shoves it into his pocket. $21.16 per week is not nearly enough. At least, it won't be in December, when he has to spend that much on light and heat alone. He chews his lower lip, thinking. All right then, he'll find extra work. He will when he needs to.

It may be that his pay is insufficient, but Bigelow has discovered something. In Alaska he is his own boss. For the first time in his life, he can order his days as he sees fit. He can build what he's seen in those minutes before he falls asleep, drawn on the red insides of his eyelids. Equations that he knows by heart, sketches he's copied onto scraps and into margins, analyses of friction impacted by velocity and altitude: a kite, a two-celled box kite that will soar above his station on the creek, whole miles higher than any kite has ever flown before. A way to understand not just the air, but the heavens.

Bigelow digs out his friend's letter, smoothes it to read the date. August 8, 1915. More than a month has passed. Already he's hired and fired the Indians. He's traded his father's watch chain and fobs for a parka with wolverine trim. He's eaten strawberries that have grown to the size of fists in the long summer light.

And he's seen the Aleut woman. He's followed her along the town's new main street.

At first he thinks she might be a deaf-mute, but she isn't deaf, because she startles at the diagnostic noises he makes, dropping an armload of wood, clattering a pan on the stove. And she isn't mute, either. She cries out in the bed, mews and moans and even, sometimes, giggles.

It is snowing on the day he follows her home. Small, dry flakes blow like dust behind the lenses of his glasses. Eleven degrees at noon, with a shifting wind, first from the west, then from the north, then west again. On his way from the cable office he breaks a bootlace, and when he bends to fix it, knotting the two ends together, it breaks in a new place. So he stops at Getz's General Merchandise.

She has three tusks of walrus ivory and a bundle of pelts, red fox mostly, pups and summer skins not worth more than a dime apiece. She leans forward over the wide counter to point at what she wants in exchange—tea, tobacco, toffee, a bottle of paregoric. Her arm up, her ungloved fingers outstretched, she waits until Getz takes each item from the shelf, slaps it down on the

counter in a manner intended to convey impatience and condescension.

At Getz's, payment is accepted in a number of forms: gold,
flake or nugget; coins, American, Russian, and Canadian; skins—
sable, marten, mink, otter, seal, rabbit, lynx, wolverine, caribou,
bear, wolf, moose, fox, lemming, beaver—anything bigger than
a rat that has a hide to tan; and miscellany, blankets, boots,
eggs, nails, needles, knives. Two walls of the store are devoted to
complications of equivalence, and while certain values are not
negotiable—gold is gold, and it is twelve dollars an ounce, this
is painted on the wall in black—the worth of an egg, for exam-
ple, goes up and down according to the number of chickens that
make it through the winter. And that population depends on
how many have worn themselves out laying without cease when
days are twenty hours long. So Getz inscribes the cost of eggs in
chalk.

"Not un—uh, ornamental," he says, noting how Bigelow
stares at the woman. With one proprietary elbow pinning down
the pelts, he ties her purchases together with twine. "If the war
paint don't bother you."

As if she understands, the woman turns and stares back at
Bigelow, her jaw thrust forward, unapologetic, even defiant. In
what way does she see him? How does he look to her? He thinks
of himself as handsome—handsome enough, anyway—with a
broad face, pale blue eyes almost too widely set, a straight nose,
and a wide mouth that balances the eyes. There's nothing sharp
in his face, nothing mean. His big forehead appears even bigger
because of his fair eyebrows, his slightly elevated hairline. As for
her: black braid, black eyes, black buttons on her bodice, and little black lines drawn on her chin. She watches Bigelow watching
her, and her pale tongue comes into the corner of her mouth.

Bigelow forgets his broken bootlace and follows her out the

door and up the frozen rut in the middle of the street. The three tins swing from her hand, now hidden in its sealskin mitten; the brown bottle gleams in the other. She walks without once looking back at him, without turning her head to the right or the left, neither slow nor fast, steps as neat as stitches, and he stumbling and slipping ten paces behind the back of her parka.

By the time she reaches her house he's caught up to her, and when she opens the door he goes in after her, sufficiently amazed by his own boldness to leave the door ajar. A dusting of snow collects in his wake. She puts her packages down on the table, picks up her broom, and sweeps the flakes outside before they have a chance to melt.

As if he were not there—her failure to acknowledge him isn't a refusal, it is nothing so pointed that he can use the word *ignore*—she hangs her mittens on a nail, she removes her parka and boots, she unties the twine from her tins of tea, tobacco, and toffee. Then she chooses a small log from the wood box, picking through its contents for the piece she wants, and opens the door of the stove to lay it on the embers.

Neither of them speaks, and if he steps in her path, she moves silently out of his way. It is perhaps a quarter of an hour before they touch, and this is only the contact required for her to remove his parka, as it is dripping on the floor. With his heart beating so that he can feel it, he watches her fingers ease the long bone buttons from the loops of leather, he holds his arms out, and the coat's heavy sleeves slide from them. She hangs the wet fur on a peg by the door, and he sits down in one of her two chairs.

From his seat by the stove he watches her make and drink a cup of tea, then unwrap the foil from around a toffee and slowly chew it. The candy is so adhesive that twice her teeth stick together. To loosen them she moves her lower jaw from side to side, frowning with the effort, and he can see muscle under the smooth skin of her cheek. When she is finished, her pale tongue again emerges, licking whatever sweetness remains on her lower lip. Then she closes her mouth and looks at him.

It's a long look, not appraising, and not inquisitive. She must know what he wants, but she betrays neither apprehension nor enthusiasm—nothing of what she feels—and he returns her gaze without any idea as to what she might be thinking. She doesn't appear to find him attractive, nor repugnant. Living on the out-skirts of town, she's seen enough whites that he can't strike her as surprising or compelling or even interesting.

After a minute, he realizes that he is trying to fill the silence with gestures, lifting and lowering his eyebrows, compressing his lips, sniffing, blinking, touching his face—the visual equivalent of chatter—and he stops.

The light from the window has dimmed. She retrieves a lamp from the shelf where she keeps her tobacco, a hurricane lamp with a spotless glass chimney, filled with fishy-smelling oil that makes the wick sputter and spark. After lighting it, she doesn't sit but remains standing behind her chair, her hands holding the top rung; and, as this posture seems to Bigelow like a dismissal, he gets to his feet. He pulls on his boots, parka, and gloves, and closes her door behind him.

He feels drunk as he walks through the early twilight, new snow creaking under his boots and the dogs just beginning to howl. His mouth is dry and his heart pounds as if from exertion, but it isn't that, it's something else. Suddenly, the streets are beautiful, glittering and blue under a sky stretched so wide it has room for everything: sun, moon, and stars.

By the time he moves from his tent into his station house, winter has arrived. November 18, 1915, the sun sets at 2:42 P.M., and Bigelow, bundled upstairs in parka, boots, and discouragingly pungent caribou trousers, watches it disappear across the inlet's sullen horizon and inscribes the hour and the minute into his log, writing as carefully as he can without removing his gloves. The sun's descent illuminates the various layers of cloud, inspiring him to annotate their features and relative positions in the sky. A single remaining ray, like a celestial finger, reaches up and points to the blurred belly of nimbostratus, and he watches as it fades. Perhaps it will snow the next day. Bigelow stands, hugging himself against the cold, until he can see no more.

Downstairs, where he can move around without the encumbrance of furs, he has placed his drafting table next to the stove, and he works at its slanting surface during the long dark hours of the season. He has his responsibilities to the central bureau in Washington, D.C., and he has local duties as well.

For the town of Anchorage, in a frenzy of construction,

Bigelow is to create a forecast map and tack it to the post office wall every day by two P.M., and he is to fly flags appropriate to that forecast: white for fair, blue for rain or snow, a red pennant for easterly winds, a yellow for westerly, and so on—eighteen combinations to cover all the possibilities, a language of signals familiar to citizens of the United States, but who knows if the local populace will understand it? Still, that isn't Bigelow's problem; his forecasts are for the Alaska Engineering Commission and its railroad, for which everyone is waiting.

There's coal in Alaska—coal fields and diamond mines, veins of gold, silver, copper—and the fastest way to get it out of the territories and sold is by rail. If President Wilson relents, if the United States joins the Allies against Germany, the war effort will demand Alaska's wealth. No one wants war, and yet everyone is excited by the possibility. Impatient to finish laying track and begin surveying for a deepwater port, the Engineering Commission has already made mistakes, mistakes for which weather was blamed, and Bigelow has been sent north to prevent more of them from happening. Last year, all the equipment shipped up from Panama's completed canal—steam shovel, dredge, and crane—sank in the inlet. An unexpected storm blew in, the wind hit fifty knots, two barges crashed into floe ice and sank. So now the commission has decreed that no work proceed before the weather forecast is known. And forecasts depend on maps. To the initiated, air has features as clear as land, features that can be drawn, lines that divide one degree from another. Interpretations of those drawings may vary, opinions among meteorologists diverge, but good maps are absolute; they are irrefutable.

The bureau provides large-scale outlines of North America, printed on both opaque and tissue-thin folios. On the opaque maps, Bigelow enters temperature and pressure readings, delineating highs and lows with isotherms and isobars, fancy words for the lines he makes, sweeping over topography in waves and circles. On the translucent overlays, he indicates wind and precipitation, using directional arrows and a code of symbols for rain, snow, sleet, and fog. He plots his own data—readings he has taken and reported to the central office—as well as observations from all the other stations in North America, numbers he decodes from a long, daily cable message. But without a light table like the one at which he worked in Seattle, he sometimes makes mistakes, and even more of them when dogs are howling. Pen in hand, he startles at the sound, rakes its nib across ten or twenty degrees of longitude.

Half wolf, three quarters wolf, all wolf—the sound of sled dogs after dinner is like nothing Bigelow has ever heard before, one howls and then another answers and so it goes until dawn. Horses aren't much use when snow is four feet deep, and the few automobiles shipped into Anchorage are good for nothing but sport—ice derbies and mud races—and the railroad isn't finished, it's barely begun. So anyone who plans on getting anywhere walks on snowshoes or travels behind a team.

When sled dogs aren't working they're staked, and Bigelow has grown accustomed to the sight of chains disappearing into the dens the dogs dig in the snow. But, invisible as the animals are when he walks through town, they fill the night with their wailing, like hideous hymns to the devil—once they begin, stars wink out and the bright moon sinks in the sky. Fingers in his ears, wool watch cap, earmuffs, parka hood: he can't find a way to muffle the howling. Even *Rigoletto*, cranked up and blaring from the trumpet, is no good, the tenor's lament threading eerily through the howling of the dogs. The death of civilization, the death of reason, it seems to Bigelow, tearing up one map and then another.

He binds the completed maps in volumes of 120 pages, each holding two months' worth of recorded observations, paths of major storms extrapolated for comparison to those of years past and hence. Current theories of forecasting presuppose that atmospheric history tends, like human history, to repeat itself, an idea that some meteorological scientists consider facile. And, sometimes, sitting by the stove, feet numb and cheeks burning, Bigelow lifts his head from his task and is struck by its absurdity. He isn't drawing mountains or rivers or canyons, all those features of the earth that have existed for aeons; and neither is he mapping countries or cities or even streets, the work of centuries. No, Bigelow records ephemera: clouds; a fall of rain or of snow; hailstones that, after their furious clatter, melt silently into the ground. Like recounting a sigh.

But there are other nights when this seems to him wonderful, poetic. He is recording a narrative that unfolds invisibly to most people, events that, even if noted, are soon forgotten. A storm such as the one that destroyed his grandmother's home might be represented in diaries and stories, but not accurately. Its character would be distorted, altered by tellings and retellings, made into a myth rather than a set of responsibly reported observations.

As with the shard of blue-and-white china he keeps, the pattern from which he can picture his grandmother's unbroken plate, after winds blow then still, after clouds vanish, only Bigelow will have the record.

SHE IS A WOMAN, and women want things. But what? What would she like? Hairpins and combs? At Getz's store, Bigelow stares at the meager stock of ladies' notions. Ipswich No. 223 cotton lisle stockings? Black? Double-soled for heavy wear? He doesn't know.

DeBevoise dress shields. Mennen's Violet Talcum Powder. Under Getz's eye, he considers each item, turning cans and crinkling packets in his hands; but he leaves the store without buying anything—anything that might be taken as an intimacy, an intimacy he hasn't been offered, rather than a gift.

Bigelow pictures the woman's house, the stove and table and chairs and shelf. What does she need? What might she use? Unable to think of anything better, he goes back to the station to retrieve what he shot that morning, a long-legged rabbit that waited too long to jump.

He walks to her house, carrying the animal first by its ears, then by its hind feet. His stomach twists, as if he's missed supper, but it's not yet four. It's because he's nervous, very nervous. A handful of women among thousands of men, and of those few, Bigelow is pursuing one he finds not merely beautiful but necessary. Necessary. Is this the effect of loneliness, of deprivation? He's warned himself against her closing the door in his face, against the sight of another man in the chair across from hers. Over and over he's told himself that either of these outcomes is far more likely than her inviting him inside. But it's done no good. And he hasn't bothered to plan what to do if she doesn't ask him in—it seems impossible that he could still exist on the other side of such disappointment.

"*Kla-how-ya,*" he practices as he walks. *Klaaa. How. Yuh.* His experience with pidgin hasn't been encouraging, but what other words can he use?

He speaks the phrase when she answers his knock, *how are you,* and he holds out the gift, the rabbit. Without taking it, she steps aside so he can enter, so she can close the door on the cold.

"*Mesika,*" he tries, pushing the animal into her hands. *Yours.* He points at her stove.

"*Com-tox?*" *You understand?* Although, inflections for *com-tox* are tricky. He may have told her that it's he who understands.

She puts the rabbit on the table. He points again at the stove, and she inclines her head a degree, nothing as much as a nod.

I'm Bigelow. I think you're beautiful. I can put my mouth on your mouth? What's your name? How are you called? I want to hold you. Will you take your—dress, dress, what's the word for dress? He's forgetting all he knew—*Can I take your clothes off?*

Bigelow gets out his Chinook dictionary. "*Be-be,*" he says, settling on something simple. *Kiss.*

The smallest of smiles, or has he imagined it? She looks where his finger points at the word and its translation.

He has imagined it. She's not smiling. But she doesn't look unhappy. She looks—what does she look? He's about to give up,

go home, when the woman moves a hand to her throat and begins with that button.

Bigelow stares as the bodice of her dress opens to show her
body underneath. She folds it, then takes off her underclothes
and folds them, too, unhurried. He follows her into the other
room, bringing the lamp so that he can see her face, search it to
confirm that this is what he hopes it is, an invitation.

She raises her eyebrows; he lifts his shirt over his head without bothering to unbutton it. Eager, not greedy. He's rehearsed
this scene more times than he can count, and he intends to be as
polite as he knows how.

But he's barely felt his way between her legs when she takes
his wrist and pulls his hand away.

Okay, he thinks, all right, and he scoots down, his legs right
off the bed, to insinuate his tongue in that spot.

She pops straight up. Grabs his ears like jug handles to remove his head from her crotch.

"What?" Bigelow says uselessly. "What do you want?"

The woman lies back down and he sits next to her, looking at
the smooth, unreadable flesh of her stomach. *"Icta?"* he translates into Chinook. *What?*

She closes her eyes and opens her legs a few inches.

He doesn't move.

She bends her knees, and he arranges himself over her body.

With one hand planted on the bed, he uses the other to guide
himself inside her, keeping his eyes on her face to make sure he's
not doing anything she doesn't like, watching the effect of each
careful thrust.

He doesn't want for her to have escaped behind the lids of
her eyes—it seems as if he can see her there, in the dark, folded
in a place too small to admit another occupant. He's getting
what he hoped, he tells himself, but it isn't at all what he ex-

pected, and a desolation seizes him. He's not joined to her, he can't reach her.

Like a key, the thought of her eluding him turns in his flesh.

He stays hard, his ears ring, a new taste floods his mouth, and he keeps moving, following the thrust of his cock, determined to find her.

WHEN HE TEARS the side of his parka, it is the woman who repairs it, unfastening the coat and taking it from his shoulders as she did on the day he followed her home, then stepping outside her door to shake the dry snow from the fur.

As he watches, she unwinds a length of heavy black thread from a spool and cuts it with her teeth before drawing it back and forth over a bar of yellow wax. Then she coaxes its end through the eye of a long needle and begins, using the heel of her hand protected by a disc of bone to push the needle through the skin. While she works, he holds the wax, rubbing his thumb over its scored surface. His eyes follow her industrious fingers. There is an impersonal quality to her labor; it seems not so much a gift to him as it does a habit of northern housewifery. Furs must be kept in repair. A torn parka, otherwise valuable, is next to useless.

Her stitches are small. The needle makes slow progress. Oddly, when its bright point emerges and then disappears back into the dark fur, he feels a tightening in his chest, and he gets up from where he is sitting silently next to her on the bed and paces, yawning and sighing, until she has finished.

Contrary to what prejudice has taught him to expect, she is not uninhibited. He's heard how native girls mature earlier than whites, how mothers and fathers send their daughters off to be initiated by uncles or friends. But she does not betray the evidence of such an education. There is a whole list of affectionate gestures she will not tolerate.

While she keeps still for a closed-mouth peck, if he attempts a more penetrating kiss she quickly turns her head, leaving him licking her cheek. She moves his hands away from her neck, her feet, her hair, and her genitals. But, once he's inside her, she lies under him with a rapt smile, eyes closed and fingers busily agitating her own flesh without regard for the rhythm he's established. When she comes, her arousal is keen—she arches her back, she cries out—but private. He cannot induce her to sit astride him or to allow him to enter her in any manner except what is understood as missionary. And perhaps this is the explanation, as the Aleutian Islands have long been colonized by Russian Orthodox.

She skins a rabbit with a grace and attention she doesn't seem to waste on him. Why doesn't he resent this? Instead he watches, intent, as she bends its ears and opens the cleft in its lip to see how young it is, how fresh. Then she girdles the skin around its hind legs and, holding its back feet in her left hand, strips the hide down over the body with her right, so that it comes off inside out, as quickly as if she were removing a glove. The parting of silver-gray fur from tender new muscle reveals an elastic integument of faintly iridescent blue, like the raiment of a ghost, and once, when he reaches out to touch it, she pulls the animal quickly from under his hands. She takes off the head and saves it with the skin, saves the entrails as well, washes and butchers the carcass. As she works, the muscles play under the smooth skin of her forearms, and otherwise invisible sinews stand out on the backs of her small hands.

Every meeting is the same, as ritual as his walks to and from the telegraph office, his entering observations into a log. He watches as she prepares the food he has brought; he eats with her in silence; they lie together on her bed, a fur blanket beneath them; he waits until she cries out and arches her back, then allows himself release.

When he lets her go, she sits up. She leaves the bed to retrieve a tin tub from behind the stove and she fills it with water left hot in her two big kettles. Then she opens her tin of tobacco, readies her pipe, and sits cross-legged, smoking in the tub while he talks to her, propped on one elbow, wondering at his gabble and yet helpless to stop it.

Later, walking home to the station or lifting his head from the work on his table, he asks himself if it is some failure on his part: the lack of spontaneity. It isn't he who imposes the order, but perhaps in some way he doesn't understand he is its catalyst.

He devises little tricks—puerile, at once irresistible and shaming. He stands on his hands and knocks at her door with his heel, he opens his mouth to reveal a button on his tongue. But this doesn't provoke her, she doesn't even blink. Instead, she removes his coat to look for the spot on his shirt from which he's torn it, she takes the button from his mouth and stitches it back, tight, where it belongs. It's as if she anticipates his nonsense and hardens herself against it.

She opens for him, yes, but only her legs, and all the rest that she does—preparing food, mending furs, even waxing his boots—strikes him as an elaborate decoy, a way of distracting him from her deeper self, her deep*est* self, all that he wants most to penetrate.

She.

Inside her is a name, a word he wants to know. To possess.

RIVERS EMPTY INTO COOK INLET: the Susitna, the Cha-
kachatna, the Matanuska, the Yentna, and others, whose native
pronunciations Bigelow hasn't yet mastered. Ringed by sand and
clay cliffs, the inlet's water is clouded in spots by swirling, silty
spirals of sediment, glacial detritus hammered by the ocean's
tide.

Exploring the land around Anchorage, searching for the ideal
place from which to launch a kite, Bigelow discovers a cove fed
by an eddying backwash. He picks his way through a litter of
splintered boats and bridges, of lost tents and snapped tent
poles, sleds and whips, the occasional drowned dog tangled in its
harness.

Spring breakup is fast, fast enough to strand wolf and caribou
on the same raft of ice. He's heard stories of hurtling floes, frozen
islands with a surface area of an acre or more speeding downriver
with tents pitched on top and campfires still burning. The cove
debris curls and bobs in a yellow lather of briny froth, deposited
on the shore, licked back into the water, then rolled onto the

beach again, hundreds of miles downstream from its sudden, accidental departure.

Snowshoes of varying degrees of workmanship. A fistful of
matches still dry in their waterproof can. A wooden tripod. A
needlepoint cat stretched taut in its frame. A broken-necked
ukulele. A statue of the Virgin with her nose sheared off, her
blue dress faded to the same limy gray-green as the water that
brought her. Two brooms and one bowling pin. A shard of mirror left in the corner of a gilt frame. An oak headboard with
carved pineapple finials. A braided switch of blond hair. A hasty
plank grave marker, the dates 1872–1911 burned onto one side.
Walking bent over along the water's edge, Bigelow examines
each object, keeping whatever seems useful, the matches and the
shard of mirror, the tripod, and two snowshoes that might work
together. He ties them on, tests their weave on the sand, thinking of his own possessions, what little he packed and brought
north. Maps and instruments, clothes, although not enough and
not the right ones, a box of books and a few sentimental trinkets,
and his work, of course, calculations—thousands of them—
copied meticulously into notebooks.

Standing on the shore, swaying on the long shoes, Bigelow
imagines these things in the water, his among what others have
lost, his maps and equations and longings erased by the tide.

To slow himself down, to give her time to come, he has to stop moving altogether.

He has to call upon his whole repertoire of calming images, one especially, he has no idea its source, of an empty chair in a road—a simple wooden chair, the kind you'd expect in a kitchen, and yet it sits alone, without table, lamp, or occupant, in the middle of a straight, paved road, a road going nowhere. Green fields on either side and a range of mountains in the distance. An altocumulus, maybe two.

Once he adds the clouds, he runs through classifications of their forms, starting with the lowest, the nearly earthbound stratus and fractostratus, up through cumulus and nimbus and all their subclassifications, even those textbook clouds that he never sees, like altocumulus-castellus, up and up through all the layers of the air until Bigelow reaches the high, high cirrus, clouds spread at thirty thousand feet like a frayed veil between earth and heaven, between coming and not coming.

Aloft, he swallows his breath, in control now, almost.

The habit of ice.

The habit of ice.

The habit of ice will hold him where he wants to be held, frozen at that most delicious point. The basic pattern of ice is hexagonal, a union of six tetrahedra, but the formation of crystals varies with temperature. From zero to negative three degrees centigrade, it is the habit of ice to form thin hexagonal plates. With the subtraction of one or two degrees, needles result. Take away three and get hollow prismatic columns. From negative eight to negative twelve: thicker hexagonal plates. The dendritic forms—fronds of ice, like botanical growth—occur from negative twelve to negative sixteen.

Bigelow keeps his eyes closed until she cries out. He wants to watch her as she comes, the way she seems for a moment to swim beneath him, her legs kicking in some rhythm he can almost understand.

But she's too quick; it's over before he has a chance to see.

"The difference between a balloon and a kite is that a balloon can be blown off course."

He sits across from her at the table as she examines the raccoon he has brought. It's still warm; he shot it in the station, cornered it under his bed, where he keeps—used to keep—his cornmeal and his sugar.

"And," he says, "to fly a balloon, you need good weather. That's not true for kites."

Her clothes are off, folded on the chair. She has only the one dress, and sometimes removes it before cutting up game. He'd like to believe this is to please or tempt him, but she's no more flirtatious than she is modest. It must be that she doesn't want to get it stained. He watches as she picks up the carcass, turns it over, looking for the place where the shot entered, a way to predict how it will bleed when she butchers it. Her breasts move with the rest of her, not so small that they don't sway prettily when she stoops to retrieve a fallen knife. Still, he knows better than to interrupt her when she's working.

"The first thing that was wrong with the Nairobi experiment

was the balloon, because balloons have no line, no line angles to measure, so they could only estimate the height, they couldn't calculate it. Besides being wasteful, because you have to send up five balloons for every one you reclaim. They just deflate. Or they burst and fall, and that's no good—not here in Alaska, the population's too sparse. Around Nairobi there's a million people who will retrieve a balloon, but here in the territories I'd never get my instruments back.

"Anyway, a kite's better. With the length of the line and the angle it presents, I can determine the exact height. It's a standard equation, Pythagorean, using a sine table for the—

"Look," he says to the woman, and he pulls her away from the table, the raccoon divided into a bowl of entrails, a pan of meat. He steps around the pelt, set fur-side down so as not to stain the floor. She'll scrape it later, after he's gone.

With a hand on either shoulder, he sits her on her bed. Then he opens his rucksack. She leans forward, curious. Has he brought another, different animal?

White fabric. He pulls it out, unfolds, unfolds, unfolds. It covers her lap, her bed, her table; it falls in rippling layers and washes up against the doorsill.

"A hundred and eighty square feet of muslin," he says. "Lifting surface. And that's just one cell's worth. Do you know how much that is?" He throws his arms open. "Six by nine by twelve. Six feet tall, nine feet long, twelve feet wide. There's never been a kite this big. Not on record." He picks up the end of the fabric and wraps it around her naked shoulders, looks at her black eyes. She indulges him for a moment, holding still before shrugging it off so that it crumples around her on the bed.

Bigelow picks up a corner. "Every night I make myself sew another seam. God, but I'm slow. I don't know how you do it. An hour every night, and not half, not a quarter as neat as you." He finds the spot where he left off and pushes it into her hands.

She examines the place, smudged gray, where his fingers gripped the cloth. The muslin is puckered in spots, and she pulls at the fabric, trying to smooth it.

"I found a tall fir. Dragged it two, maybe two and a half miles to the mill and had it cut. Thirty-four spars. The kite takes twenty-eight, but they can crack, sometimes they break in flight. And I'm nowhere near finished sanding.

"Here's what I need," he says. "I need to build a reel that includes some kind of timing device. A stationary reel that I can set to pause at five-, maybe ten-minute intervals. Then instruments can record at selected altitudes. The Nairobi balloon, it was—well, it was famous. Written up in all the papers . . ." Bigelow trails off.

"What I need," he says after a minute, "is line that's strong enough to go up for miles. And a reel that's bolted down to some kind of platform. Because you can't control a kite this big. Not manually. It would pull you off your feet."

The woman hands the muslin back to Bigelow, and he sees a fleck of blood on it, from her hands.

"Silk. I thought silk," he says. "But silk might fray on a reel. So it's got to be metal, but flexible. Piano wire. Maybe that would work.

"It's going to change everything. Forecasts—it will make long-range forecasts possible."

He folds the muslin, folds it tight to fit back inside his rucksack. "See," he says, laying the bag aside, "what they did in Nairobi was measure the air temperature over the equator. And found out that it isn't hot."

He takes her fingers and gives them a shake. "It isn't even warm," he says. "It's *cold*. Cold the way you'd expect air to be here. *Freezing*."

Bigelow releases the woman. He throws himself back on her bed, chewing his lower lip, thinking. "Everyone knows that winds move eastward around the globe, because of the earth, the rotating earth. That's obvious. But it's also true that heat rises." He gets up, walks to the stove, holds a hand above its surface. "So you'd think air over the equator would be hot. Hot like it is near the ground. I mean, Nairobi! But. But."

Bigelow steps out of his boots and onto the chair, and from chair to table, avoiding the bloody bowl and the knife. He reaches to feel the air near the ceiling, jumps down before she can begin to scold. While she watches, he moves the chair from one part of the room to another, standing on its seat to test the air overhead. Then he sits down next to her with his pen and notebook and sketches her square room, floor, walls, stove, and ceiling. "See," he says, and he draws arrows coming up out of the stove, arrows that move toward the middle of the ceiling and down the opposite wall, across the floor and back, big, spiraling circles. "That's the way a closed system of air circulates."

He pulls her up from the bed and walks her through the room. "Warm. Cold. Warm. The earth, it's a closed system, too. Heat from the equator rises. Cold air from the poles sinks. And it would make huge crosscurrents. Streams that flow across east–west winds."

The woman stands back, watches Bigelow sweep his arms around. "I bet," he says, "that the air over Anchorage is warmer than the air over Nairobi. I just have to get the kite high enough."

The woman looks at him, her eyebrows drawn together. He's made her forget the raccoon.

"You'll see," he says. "You'll come with me, up the bluff. I have a place picked out. A spot where the wind is always perfect.

"The kite, it's going to be huge. Enormous. This"—he picks up the rucksack with the fabric inside—"this is just to give you an idea. It isn't even half of it. A kite big enough to carry all the instruments you could want. Barometer, thermometer, anemometer, hygrometer." He ticks them off on his fingers. "Dry-cell battery, and rotating barrel for graphing readings simultaneously."

She sits on her bed, leaning back on her elbows, and he comes to her. He kneels and puts his arms around her waist.

"You'll come with me, up to the place I've found," he tells her. And he tries, because he can't not try, to get his tongue between her legs.

He brings her a bar of soap. He likes to think of her, sitting in the bath.

There isn't much of a selection, not in a place like Anchorage, not in April, when the inlet's ice pack still prohibits shipping, but still, he lingers over the available brands. Canthrox, one bar says—shampoo. He's never seen her wash or even wet her shining hair. Cuticura, but he doesn't like its medicinal name or its smell. Naphtha, for laundry only. Most of the soaps have been on the shelf long enough that their wrappers are stained and torn. After all, why buy soap when most people bathe at a bathhouse and bathhouses provide their own?

Bigelow returns to the one bar with a picture on its label: a lady in a tub, her ringed hand resting on its edge, bubbles floating up from the surface of the water. The bathtub is long and has claw feet. It isn't much like the one the woman uses. And the woman isn't much like his woman, either. She has a little cap on her head, with curls peeping out from under. LAVANDE. The word is written under the drawing. French. On the other side of the wrapper is the address of the National Toilet Company in Paris, Tennessee.

Still, if she likes the pictures of the corsets, the dimpled faces above the squeezed middles.

Bigelow buys the soap, and after they eat and lie together in the bed, he gives it to her. She's sitting in the tin tub, smoking, and he slips out from under the skins to fetch the bar from his coat.

"Here," he says, and she takes it from him. She lays the pipe on the floor beside the tub and, using both hands, turns the gift over and over, smells it, looks once more at the picture, then hands it back.

"No," he says. "It's for you. For baths." He unwraps the soap and gives it to her, and immediately it slips from her wet hand into the water, where she leaves it.

Bigelow hesitates for a moment, then puts his hand in and fishes around for the bar. Past an ankle, under a thigh, the surprise of pubic hair, crisp and springy, even underwater. He hesitates too long in that spot, and she takes his wrist, she pulls his hand from the tub. But he's seen the soap's shadow; before she can stop him, he has it and is rubbing the bar up and down her arm to demonstrate how it makes lather, sniffing at it to show her its perfume.

She doesn't like it. She gets out of the water and empties the tub out the door. Still naked, she fills the kettle with snow and puts it back on the stove, sits in the chair to wait for hot water while Bigelow gathers his clothes and dresses, taking his time because the sight of her perched there, nothing on, is one he enjoys. Too proud to cover herself, she'd rather be cold, the dusky skin of her breasts almost mauve, their nipples drawn up in angry, hard points.

The next time he's at her place he sees that the soap is gone—she's thrown it away, no doubt. But she's kept the wrapper. She's stuck it to the wall as decoration.

So he's gotten something right after all.

As it would make no sense to assemble and disassemble a kite of such complexity and proportion, Bigelow is building a shed for it on the bluff, and, outside the shed, a platform on which to mount a reel. He has lumber left over from the construction of the station house, and he has bought a box of cheap, bent nails from Getz.

On days he does not see the woman, he spends his afternoons on the bluff. He straightens nails with a hammer, striking sparks from the flat rock where he pounds them. He frames the shed and he puts up walls, he pitches the roof steeply to prevent snow from sticking.

Then he carries all the kite's pieces from the station up to the shed, making two trips with a sledge, first the spars and the wing ribs, and the next day all the rest, muslin and tools and the instruments he wants to send up into the sky.

Inside the new building, protected from the wind, he begins to put the kite together. Crouched under a hurricane lamp tied to a beam, Bigelow is so involved, day after day, with the details of the work at hand—box corners and lock slots, lengths of hemp soaked and tied wet so as not to loosen in flight, spars, three of them, that crack under tension and have to be replaced, a seam so crooked it has to be resewn—that he doesn't see the whole of what he's making.

Not until it's done, ribs tight, stitches knotted. Bigger somehow than he expected. Grander and more beautiful, with a grace that drawings can't convey.

He walks around and around the kite, squeezing to fit between the taut muslin panels of the cells and the plank sides of the shed, running his fingers over the fabric, touching spars that he sanded, one each night in his station, until they were as smooth as her skin.

He can't wait to get it outside, into the wind.

ALL WEEK HE HAS no luck with his gun: torrents of rain wash every last bird from the sky, the rabbits are deep in their dens. Soon the mosquitoes will be as fierce as when he arrived. With nothing to offer the woman, and unable to face the idea of a long, wet evening spent alone, Bigelow settles on the idea of some netting for her bed; he walks into town to buy a bolt from Getz's store.

His purchase held inside his coat to keep it dry, he's heading east toward her house, when he sees a man crossing Front Street with a mixed brace slung over his shoulder, one scaup and another, bigger bird with a red breast. Bigelow runs through the rain to catch up with him. He wants the prettier one—a merganser, the man says it's called—but the man won't sell it for less than a quarter, so Bigelow takes the scaup instead, and then he has two gifts.

He hurries, head down, trying to avoid the deeper puddles, but by the time he arrives he's soaked through, and she makes him wait by the door, where she sets aside the bolt of netting to strip off his coat and his boots.

"Against the bugs," he says, pointing at the netting. He pan-tomimes getting bitten, slaps at his forearm and then scratches the same spot. The woman nods, a brisk gesture, eyebrows raised as if to say she's not so ignorant—so savage—that she doesn't recognize mosquito netting.

He stands barefoot on her bed to screw a ring into the ceiling, shows her how to thread the netting through it, how to drape the stuff so the bugs can't get in. When he mimes using a needle and thread to close the seam at the head of the bed, she nods, again with a kind of put-upon patience.

"Okay," he says. "Sorry," he says. Why doesn't he learn to re-sist these gestures she finds condescending?

It's pretty under the net, the way it makes filmy, indistinct shapes of the chair, the doorway, the squat black stove. The fab-ric draws halos around lamp and window, and he puts his arm around the woman. With his other hand, he tries to direct her face toward his. But she won't stay there with him. Instead, she slips out of his arms and pulls the net down, she folds it into something resembling the original bolt.

He moves back to the other room, gets the duck and lays it on the table, sits by the stove, feeling suddenly cold and cheap, apologetic on account of its pedestrian black-and-white feathers. But then she never saw the other one, with the tufted green head, the blood-colored breast.

She undresses before the lamp, and her naked shadow falls across the table, spills into his empty lap.

She picks up the bird, examines it minutely, as she does every meal he brings. There's no reason to assume she can tell he hasn't bagged the scaup himself, and yet Bigelow feels sure she knows it isn't his. Except, he tells himself, that it is. He did buy it, after all. He gave the man what he had left in his pocket, one dime and one nickel.

She cuts the neck to let it bleed; then, without plucking any feathers, she skins it. Does she find the plumage pretty enough to preserve intact? She opens the stomach to find what's there: the orangy flesh of a bivalve and two small crabs, whole, their legs folded tight. Bigelow finds the sight of them sad somehow, as if rather than having been eaten, they'd been put carefully away, saved for some purpose.

He will think of the crabs later. He'll try to see them as they were, the pair of them, legs pulled into their sides. He'll close his eyes to better remember each detail of this evening—the halos drawn by the netting, the smear of blood on the table, the coat of feathers drying on a nail. He'll wish he'd paid closer attention, as he surely would have had he known to look for auguries. Had he known she would leave him.

As it is, he just sits, shivering by the stove. The scaup has a fishy taste, but he eats it, he holds out his plate for more, the only way he knows to compliment her.

THE DISAPPEARANCE of the Aleut woman grieves him as nothing ever has. "I'm dying," he tells the face in his shaving mirror. He expects the words to embarrass him, to rouse him from self-pity, but they feel true.

He reminds himself that he has lists of what he's learned to do without: butter, milk, peach cobbler. Newspapers, paving stones. A decent library, and a place to buy new recordings for his gramophone. A hot bath in his own home instead of a threadbare gray towel and ten shavings of soap for a penny at one of the bathhouses.

And he has always been restrained in the expression of emotion. He didn't cry when his father died, not even when the undertaker and his boy carried the corpse feetfirst from the bedroom, down the stairs, and into the road. After the funeral, Bigelow's mother gave him a box of his father's effects. That was the word she used, *effects,* and he remembers repeating the two syllables silently to himself, over and over, *e-ffects, e-ffects,* a compulsive mental throat clearing, but one that produced no result, for he never opened the box. He noted its size, and imagined what a container of its dimensions might hold—eyeglasses, cuff links, the sign, B. GREENE, ATTORNEY AT LAW, that had hung under the bell—but he didn't open it.

So why, then, does he return to the woman's abandoned house almost daily, driven to reconsider the two vacant rooms, the window's empty pane of light as it moves across the floor and onto the opposite wall?

Sunday morning hours that he once squandered in church, crammed into a pew between mother and sister, grudgingly dropping nickels into the collection plate, he spends in rooms she has consecrated, a word that surprises him when it comes into his head. *Consecrated.* After all, he hasn't been to a Sunday service in ten years. But how else to describe what he feels as he walks through her house, around and around, reeling with loneliness?

She chinked between the shrinking, warped boards of the house with scraps of leather, moss, paper—whatever came to hand—and in her absence these have fallen out and cracks have appeared, admitting air, light. He tries to restuff them, but the dried moss crumbles at his touch, the bits of leather and paper slip straight through and outside, then blow away. He presses his eye to the crack, watching the wind tease them over the packed dirt.

JULY 4, the town explodes, bunting and baseball and smuggled bottles of beer. Despite the fact that the Engineering Commission has designated the town as dry—there are no legal intoxicants in Anchorage, and anyone caught selling contraband beer or whiskey within the town site will forfeit his or her claim to a plot of land—alcohol flows through its streets from the Line, as the straggling track of whorehouses southeast of the site is called. The madams use their connections to buy beer by the crate straight off the dock, packed in boxes labeled BEANS or MOLASSES or LAUNDRY SOAP; and stills abound in the uncut woods. Women who sell their favors sell bootleg, too, either as an aphrodisiac to be consumed on the premises, or as a nightcap, to carry home in a hair-oil bottle.

Thieving and brawling among the workers hold the attention of a police force of two, without either officer troubling himself to cross Ninth Street to begin arresting prostitutes; and anyway, where would he put them? There's no jail, just a dugout under the cabin that serves as a police station. How would it look if a pair of bachelor officers were to cram a dozen or more fancy ladies into that muddy hole? So whoever wants to drink, drinks openly, especially on a summer holiday.

Bigelow watches the First Annual Sled Dog Parade. Hands shoved in his pockets, he counts forty-two teams. Even the dogs look intoxicated, all pant and slobber, snapping at one another's red, white, and blue ribbons, holding up their procession to drop back on their haunches and howl at the trombone. Abruptly, a bandstand has replaced a grove of unpulled stumps, such overnight substitutions feasible when days are twenty hours long. Bigelow wonders if all the patriotic fervor isn't a lingering effect of the solstice, just ten days past, or maybe it's that Alaska is only a territory and not a state, her every citizen necessarily, and nostalgically, far from home.

Black flies and mosquitoes are thick; citronella oil does nothing to discourage them. The crowd from the miners-versus-railroad baseball game washes around him, slapping at bugs, laughing and jostling and hurrying on to the next amusement, a ladies' nail-driving contest, planks set up on barrels and sawhorses in front of Getz's store.

Bigelow follows the crowd. At least he can get a look at a girl. "Speed and accuracy. Speed and accuracy. Only ten cents." Getz stands on a box, accepting dimes from whoever cares to try: the pastor's wife and, judging from their bright lips and tight clothes, two girls from the Line, a dozen big-armed laundresses, along with the woman who sells water from a cart.

"Skill, not luck. Ten cents to prove yourself," Getz says, and the schoolteacher steps forward.

"Hey," Bigelow calls out, and he waves. She's got bad skin, but her hair is nice, her smile is pretty. She's talked to him at Getz's store. She waves back.

"What's the prize?" Bigelow asks.

"The prize?" Getz licks his front teeth, and for a moment

Bigelow can see the bluish underside of his tongue, then it's gone. "Winning's the prize," he says.

The women stand on either side of the planks provided. Twenty-three of them, because twenty-three is how many hammers Getz has to lend. Bigelow watches the pastor's wife fill her mouth with nails, line them up like sewing pins between her lips.

"Are you ready, ladies?" Getz asks, and he asks again, "Ladies, are you ready?" There's a final jostle for elbow room as he begins to count backward from ten. "... nine ... eight ..." Counting slowly, because, as he knows, the men aren't finished laying bets, they've hardly begun. "Speed and accuracy," Getz interjects, drawing the words out, *s p e e e e d a n d* "... se - ven ... six ..."

Bigelow pushes his way through the crowd of men laying money on a barrel. "A dollar on the schoolteacher," he says, loudly enough that she can hear. Immediately he's pushed aside by a notably well-dressed man, one of the town's undertakers. "Ten dollars on that one," the undertaker says, pointing to the prettier prostitute, and he counts the bet out with clean hands.

The men laugh and catcall; they tip flasks to their mouths. But the women, they're hot and nervous, sober and determined. Their hair curls in wet tendrils, and dark, solemn stains spread under their arms. Clenched in the hot crowd of bodies, Bigelow has an erection.

"Three ... two-o-o-o ..."

"One!" Funny what you can, and can't, tell by looking at a woman. The pastor's wife with her tidy row of nails waiting between pursed lips—she can't hit the head of one to save her life. The prostitutes swing in perfect time; their arms rise and fall and strike, five hits to sink a nail completely, then on to the next, a dead heat between them and the sounds of their hammers converge into one, at least Bigelow thinks they do. The noise of twenty-three hammers makes strange, confusing music, rows of arms pumping like legs in a stage revue, an under-rehearsed can-can, moments of synchronicity giving way to scattered shots and bruised cries. Two thumbs squashed, then a third and a fourth, their owners disqualified. The laundresses are strong but slow; too often they stop to wipe wet palms on their skirts. One of the prostitutes thinks she's finished but comes up three nails short, complaining to Getz; and the winner is either the schoolteacher or the other, prettier whore.

The way the schoolteacher can hit nails is almost unseemly, certainly unladylike; all of her body gathers into the motion, and her hammer snaps through the swarming air, stings the nail heads, and claps echoes off the opposite storefront; just three more blows, faster, faster, faster: a tie, and an immediate brawl among the gamblers.

Getz laughs as the prostitute is lifted out of the fray and into the arms of the undertaker. She kisses him with her tongue, in public, in daylight. Bigelow tries to get close to the schoolteacher, a homely girl with a throng of admirers. "Can I buy you dinner?" he says, too late. A man with a weedy bunch of daisies has her by the elbow.

Bigelow's testicles ache as he watches them walk off, a complicated ache, both disappointment and relief.

AUGUST. The air is filled with migrating birds, some so high they look like handfuls of pepper tossed into the wind, others low enough that their cries deafen him. Geese fly at the top floor's big windows, mistaking reflected sky for the real thing. Those that are only stunned fall to the ground, where they lie on their sides paddling their webbed feet with helpless, convulsive jerks. Once upright, they flap and shake their heads and stumble in circles before heading down to the water to take off and rejoin their flock. Others break their necks and die. Without raising his gun, Bigelow has a surplus of game to trade in town for flour, salt, sugar, tea.

Not that he is any good at cooking. Whatever he touches turns out tough and tasteless. He doesn't have the knack of his stove, which burns the crusts of loaves and leaves the middles raw and gray. Sitting alone, chewing, his mind wanders from the book in his lap. Unbidden, the smooth skin of her arms, the spiral of her navel, the enigmatic lines on her chin: all of these return to him. He puts down his fork and rubs the pad of his thumb against those of his fingers, remembering the feel of one of her coarse hairs between them.

Without the Aleut—and without the promise of her, the excitement of a glimpse that characterized his first months in town—he finds himself prey to anxieties about his situation, worrying about money and food and especially about the coming winter, daylight whose brevity he will be forced to note in one of his logs. Darkness that will not, this time, be relieved by her company, the lamp that cast their shadows on the wall behind the bed.

To supplement his government stipend, he is teaching himself to set wire snares and to skin the animals he catches. If he can master these skills, they will guarantee a subsistence. But he has limited luck with the snares, and each time he goes to buy a trap he ends up putting it back on the shelf. Bigger prey brings higher prices, and a bounty has been set on wolves; still, he is unable to imagine the blow required to finish off a trapped animal without marring its pelt.

"Right here," Getz tells him, pointing to the spot where his own eyebrows meet. "With the butt of your rifle."

Walking through the town, making his errands last as long as possible, he notices as if for the first time how few women there are in Anchorage. Nearly three thousand men and, according to a pool hall tally, 486 females, a few of whom are seamstresses and laundresses and cooks, as well as a nurse, a singer, the schoolteacher, and the missionary's wife—his second, as one has already fled south from the rigors of high latitude. The rest are waitresses or prostitutes or natives or, frequently, a combination thereof.

To address the problem of desire, to mark the end of a day, to fall asleep, Bigelow does as he used to do—he masturbates—but having grown dependent on the woman's company, physical release now comes at psychic cost: the act only makes his loneliness more acute. It makes him feel pathetic, as it didn't used to do. He's resisted spending his limited money on prostitutes, put off by the peculiar names of the women in the parlor of the whorehouses he tries not to visit: Moosehide Annie, Bunch Grass, Nellie the Pig. He doesn't like the forthright negotiation that precedes the encounter. This is hypocritical, perhaps; he tells himself that in one sense the Aleut woman traded her favors for the meat he brought, and what is the difference between that and money? Didn't he impose himself on her just as surely as he will impose himself on Violet, the girl he chooses not for her face or figure but for her name—the only one he can say out loud without embarrassment.

He follows her up the stairs and sits on her bed, feeling oddly listless as she makes a performance of removing her blouse and stockings.

"Do you like them on or off?" she says, gesturing at her garters, and he shrugs, struck silent in the face of her loquacity, as if it is he now who must be mute. But Violet goes on, she talks about the telephone exchange the town is planning, about her sister in Vancouver who works a switchboard, about her other sister who is blind in one eye. What does he think will happen to the new sewers when it freezes, she wants to know, and isn't it a shame that the crop that does so well here is cabbage? What's the use of a cabbage that weighs seventy pounds? Does he like coleslaw?

All the while she talks she is slipping her hand between the buttons of his shirt and caressing the back of his neck. Is this what it was like for the Aleut woman as he went on and on about water tables and rain gauges and broken anemometers? At least, he thinks, she didn't understand him.

The girl's words pelt Bigelow like a fine hail of irritations, and he considers asking her to stop talking, but seeing the anxiety his silence inspires and how earnest she looks in her attempts to seduce him, he says nothing and instead closes his eyes. He's young enough that arousal doesn't require expertise, and it's over well within the half hour allotted. He sits up to watch her gather her clothes and dress. Between stockings, she opens her mouth but, perhaps finally oppressed by his refusal to converse, closes it without saying anything. If he had money to spare he would tip her extravagantly enough that she couldn't interpret his silence as disappointment, but as it is he just leaves, his hand still in his pocket, folding and unfolding the bills that remain.

Back at the station, he records the pressure, which has fallen a tenth of an inch, from 29.90 to 29.80, and the temperatures, earth 59, air 53. He looks up from the louvered shed and sees a man standing on the lip of the creek, appearing, in the distance, as tiny as a comma on a page. So small that Bigelow is struck, suddenly, by the enormous distances he has traveled. How far he is from mother and sister in St. Louis. From Chicago. Seattle. How is it that he's never considered this before?

By the time he closes his log and returns it to its shelf, night is pressing on the windows. When he lights a lamp, the panes show him his solitary reflection as it moves from stove to table and back to stove. He has no appetite, and no energy, either, so he adds four teaspoons of sugar to a tin mug of tea before sitting to work at his drafting table. He begins drawing but is distracted by a sensation—not pain exactly—at the tip of his penis, and the accompanying notion that, despite having stopped at a bathhouse afterward, already a disease is taking hold. He shifts in his chair, and the feeling fades, but not the anxiety. It isn't cold enough to require gloves, but his fingers behave as if they are numb. Twice he drops his pen, and the second time it spatters and ruins his map.

In bed, he yawns and yawns, more deeply each time but without satisfaction. And when at last he falls asleep, it is to the memory of watching her sewing his furs, the needle sharp and glinting in her fingers, slipping in and out, darting among the luster of the dark hairs.

Hᴇ ᴅɪᴅɴ'ᴛ ᴄʀʏ when his father died.

"Say good-bye," his mother told him, and he followed her into the bedroom. The shades were drawn, but the sun found its way through the cracks.

"Why is that there?" he asked, pointing to the white cloth tied under his father's jaw and over the top of his head.

"To keep his mouth from . . ." She didn't finish.

"From what?" he asked.

"Opening."

His mother sent him to his grandmother's. The idea was that he would stay there for as long as it took his mother to turn their home into a boardinghouse. Otherwise, where would the money come from? It was a big enough house, five stories, with his father's law office on the street level, a parlor and kitchen above, and bedrooms on up. By the time she finished with it, she said, the three of them—Bigelow, his mother and sister—would live in what had been the law office; all the rest would be boarders. But in the meantime he had to stay with his grandmother.

"Why doesn't she have to go?" he asked, referring to his sister.

"Because I need her."

What about me? he thought.

She packed his trousers and shirts into a valise and told him to be a help to his grandmother. He was to do whatever his grandmother said.

The train from St. Louis to Joplin took four hours, including stops. He had two slices of bread with butter spread between them, and his mother bought him a packet of sugared almonds and a bottle of ginger beer from a man on the platform. He was eleven years old, but when the woman sitting across from him in the compartment asked, he lied and said he was thirteen.

He still thinks of that lie, remembers it with shame, dishonesty not being among his usual childish failings. It must have been that thirteen represented something to him, safety, the safety of distance. Why, at thirteen, he'd be two years past all this trouble. At thirteen, he might understand what had happened to him, to all of them, his mother, his sister, himself.

"You don't look thirteen," the woman said.

"Well," Bigelow adjusted the lie. "I will be next month."

The train pulled out with a squeal and a jerk, and the bread in its wax paper slipped onto the floor. The woman picked it up.

"I'm going there because my father died." Bigelow tried out the information, testing its power. Would it silence her? It did, and it got him the window seat as well, so he spent the rest of the trip looking out at the fields, the occasional shed or stream or horse. Averting his dry eyes from her gaze.

He was supposed to be a help, but there was something the matter with him in the country. He wheezed all the time, and his grandmother put him to bed. When the twister came, neither of them could get the cellar door unlatched, it was swollen tight with rain, and she got under the covers with him, shoes and all, and they watched windowpanes break and the curtains blow flat against the ceiling. It was true what they said about twister weather; the light was green.

Because she wasn't frightened, he wasn't, either. She told him stories about past storms: chickens dropping naked from the sky, alive, with every last feather torn off; a field planted with a burst sack of seed corn, not in rows, of course, but, "tidy," she said, "you'd be surprised how tidy and even." To hear her talk it was as if tornadoes were invented for amusement, the redistribution of tools and toys, improvements in landscaping.

"Good," she said the next day, looking into the hole where the cottonwood had been. "I never liked that tree. Took up too much sun, and now I can plant flowers closer to the house."

The dust was so bad that Bigelow could hardly breathe, but he picked up shingles and shards of glass, he swept and stacked and helped her hang her gate back on its post. "I'm all right," he told his grandmother, but she made him lie down in the parlor.

She gave him the almanac to read, and he looked up the date of the twister. *Fair skies return,* it said, and it called the day *favorable for planting root crops* and reminded readers to set their strawberry plants. He showed her the page and she laughed.

"There's not a soul who can predict the weather," she said.

On the farm down the road, a man had died, tossed with tables and chairs into the hungry sky. He came down, and they put him in a box and put the box on a wagon. Bigelow and his grandmother came to the gate and watched the wagon go by. A woman was driving, holding the reins in her white church gloves. Sitting next to the box were the man's three children, silent and scrubbed, wearing their best clothes.

"They have no shoes," Bigelow said, referring to the children. He pulled at his grandmother's sleeve. "How can they go without shoes?" He tried to imagine himself, barefoot, at his father's funeral. His mother's gloves were dark gray, almost black, with three buttons at the wrist. He'd watched how she held her hands absolutely still; they didn't move at all.

His grandmother didn't say anything. Behind the wagon's wheels, dust rose and then settled.

He saw his grandmother without clothes. He still remembers that. It was late and she thought he was asleep, she didn't shut the door to her room. She was skinny and wrinkly and didn't seem to have a proper backside, and immediately he confused her with the rain of plucked chickens.

Even now he can't think of her without seeing her drop naked from above.

THE DAY BIGELOW CHOOSES for the maiden flight, September 8, is so warm he walks up the bluff without a coat, wading through high yellow grass, carrying a handheld anemometer in a rucksack on his back, as well as theodolite, pen, and his field book in which to record notes—wind speeds, line lengths, angles of incidence. With these numbers, and factoring in the curve of the line based on the speed of the wind, he'll use a sine table to estimate the height his kite reaches.

The shed and launch platform look sturdy, and Bigelow congratulates himself on their construction, all those nails pounded straight on the rock outside the station door. The reel isn't finished, and the piano wire he ordered has yet to arrive. He won't send up instruments, because what's the point? He doesn't have what he needs to get the kite high enough to collect data.

What he does have is gut, the same that the island people use for fishing. Not smooth like the strings of a tennis racket or a fiddle, but strong—it bears the weight of a seal fighting for its life. And it's cheap. Bigelow buys several thousand feet worth, testing each inch, running the oily lengths of it through his fingers, holding down one end with the toe of his boot and pulling as hard as he can on the other, tying and retying the knots. He uses red paint to mark off each hundred feet, and then spools the whole fishy-smelling, lumpy expanse onto a windlass that he's secured to the launch platform. Good enough for a trial ascent, anyway. How much longer can he wait? The kite's been assembled, locked in the shed, for nearly two months.

When he gets the thing out, he has to hold it tight—so buoyant, it wants to be off. Lucky he had the foresight to adjust the leg lines while it was still inside, sheltered from the breeze, otherwise he'd never be able to tie a decent knot. To roll it in and out of the shed he's attached bicycle wheels to the bottom corners of the aft cell. Mismatched, they work well enough, each held with a cotter pin that he can easily remove.

The kite jerks Bigelow away from the platform and onto the bluff, pulling his feet out from under him. He struggles to keep it on the ground to double-check the leads, the angle the harness presents to the wind. But why bother to consider physics? Without encouragement, the air takes the kite from his hands. He's looking around for the best point from which to release the counterweight and pace out a few yards of line, when it sails up as if enchanted, carrying seventeen pounds of ballast with it.

The clumsy windlass unwinds; the boards of the platform creak; oily, lumpy gut slithers through his guiding hands—they must be hurting, but Bigelow doesn't feel them, consumed by the ecstatic rise of the kite. So graceful, so assured and swift. Watching it, he forgets to make note of line length, doesn't bother to measure angles.

What is it that tugs at him, as if it were his heart itself unspooling? One minute the kite is before his face, large enough to blot out the rest of creation; the next it is far, far away. A handful of sticks, a shroud of white linen, the conceit of altitude. Flight.

Up in the sky, all the line played out, it appears as a little house: white and perfect. The sun ignites one of the faces of the forward cell, makes it so burningly bright that he can't look at it for long, can't watch it fly the way he wants to. Yet neither can he look away.

Bigelow touches the line to feel it again, the tremble—unlike anything else—the pull on the end of the line. Alive.

Amazing that this thing he built should fly so perfectly, so absolutely horizontal and steady, resting on an invisible current of air.

But why is he surprised? He has pages of calculations relating lift to the sine of the angle of incidence, pages more on the ratio of inertia to viscous forces. He's plotted everything out on paper with variable dihedrals, going a half degree at a time from thirty-two to thirty-eight degrees—and graphs of drag coefficients, of lift coefficients, of laminar versus turbulent wake. It isn't magic, after all, it's science.

So how to explain the effect on him of the one white face, so bright, like sunlight on the surface of the sea, throwing spangles into the air? How to explain the catch in his chest, the sudden spill of tears?

THIS TIME, when Bigelow pushes his way into her house, he sees that a silvery-green patina of lichen has spread over the surface of her door, and pretty as this is, the sight makes him desperate, it marks the passage of time. How long has she been gone? No longer weeks or even months: a season. So he is all the more surprised by the warm air inside the house, by the sight of a stove where hers had always been, a table, a chair, a bed piled with furs. Tea and tobacco on the shelf, a glass of water on the table, half full, grease fogging its surface. At last, she has come back!

He picks the water up, remembering the sheen on the woman's mouth as she ate. Is it because she never spoke that such details have assumed importance? Bigelow slowly tips the glass so that the water rolls up to its lip, then rights it. The grease hangs on its side before slipping back down. He drinks the water and replaces the empty glass on the table, sits in the chair to await the woman's return, imagining the errands that might occupy her.

The longer she is gone, the more he is tempted to go out and find her, but small as the town is, they might miss each other, so he waits. He sits, he paces, and at last decides to lie down on the bed, a presumption he hopes won't offend her, but he is suddenly so tired—it must be an effect of excitement—he can't hold himself upright in her straight-backed chair.

She has a new skin, a wolf, and the bed frame is new as well. She must have traded the old one with its creaks and groans, its one short leg.

The force of desire, the effects of loneliness, the toll of displacement: all of these are so strong that Bigelow never considers the more likely possibility, that the house has a new occupant, with a new bed. Under his cheek the smell of wolf is unfamiliar, but he falls asleep quickly, lying on his side, his knees drawn up.

In the dream, he dismembers her. It's easy enough; he's learned from watching her skin and cut up game. And there is no blood. Instead, a stream of writing spills from her veins, letters and runes and symbols he doesn't understand. They pour out in order, like a Weather Bureau teletype, a cipher he is to translate into meaning.

Except he can't fathom the writing inside the woman. He's killed her for nothing.

Bigelow wakes disoriented from the nightmare, reassuring himself that he can't have killed her, for people bleed blood, not language, and where is the knife he used?

A lamp is burning on the table, and a man sits in the chair watching him. His arm balances on the stock of a shotgun. "Have a good rest?" he says, when Bigelow doesn't explain himself.

"What are you doing?" Bigelow answers.

"What am I doing?" The man is older than Bigelow, with a

typically Alaskan beard, unbarbered and grizzled, his left eyebrow jigged through by a scar that continues up to his hairline.

"What have you done to her?"

"What've I done to who?" He leans forward, a posture more curious than predatory, and Bigelow, still suffering the effects of his dream, stands and points at the bed he was lying on.

"Her," he says. "She. The woman—her bed. The woman who lies here."

"There isn't a woman that lies there. Wish there was," he adds.

"There is. It's hers. The tobacco. The kettle." Bigelow points at things, and each time the man shakes his head. "Mine," he says each time, until finally Bigelow understands. The woman hasn't returned.

He makes an abrupt lunge for the door, but the man blocks his escape, and the two of them stand together, close enough to embrace. Bigelow, too ashamed to speak, looks at the floor. Slowly—slowly enough that, were he to try, Bigelow could elude him—the man reaches out and takes hold of the front of Bigelow's shirt, making him aware of how his heart is pounding under the fabric.

The man holds him like that until he can feel Bigelow's humiliation, until Bigelow, defeated, allows himself to sag inside his clothes. Then the man pushes him backward out the door.

STANDING ON THE BLUFF as the line plays out, peering up into the limitless and empty sky, he feels he can't catch his breath. He sinks to his knees and turns his face from the vastness above him.

Caruso sings, outsings wind scraping over rocks. Bigelow has carried his gramophone up the hill for company, a human voice, loud and triumphant, even if the language isn't one he understands.

But it's not working. Kneeling on the ground, eyes closed, panting as if he's been running, he can't stop himself—he wonders where she is, and why she left him.

NOVEMBER 19, 1916: 13 degrees; barometer 29.90, falling; .09 precip, Wind: ESE 22 mph. November 30, 1916: 13 degrees; barometer 30.00, falling, Trc. precip, W: NE 27 mph. December 2, 1916: 2 degrees; barometer 29.80, falling, 1.02 precip, W: 0 mph. December 17, 1917: –4 degrees, barometer 29.60, falling. 0 precip. W: SE 3.5 mph.

Barometer falling, barometer falling. How can it be that the barometer is always falling? Wouldn't it have to rise sometimes? Years later, remembering his second winter in Anchorage, Bigelow's impression will be that the pressure continued impossibly to plummet, and that the long nights were (every one of them, despite notations to the contrary) unrelieved by the rising of the moon or the appearance of stars.

He uses more kerosene than he can afford, buying extra lamps and keeping a circle of them burning around his table as he works, getting up to crank the gramophone, to set the kettle to boil, to stamp his feet, change his gloves, examine his bloodshot eyes in the mirror propped above the basin—anything to distract him from solitary nights twenty hours long. Inside his moat of light, the maps he draws have the smudged and amateurish look of those he produced as a novice, their quality sacrificed to disruption, inattention, his sudden inability to sit and focus as the work requires.

But what does it matter? Tracking storms in order to forecast the weather: isn't this just another conceit? If hail destroys crops, if drought produces fires, if another hundred ships are lapped up by the tides—well, tragedy is humankind's one talent. Without elements to oppose, they invent their own disasters. Look at Europe, digging herself into rat-infested trenches.

Bigelow paces and sighs and yawns. He opens the door to the stove and kneels to watch as a log collapses into coals, sits on the floor with his chin propped on his knee and lays out game after game of solitaire, never winning but starting over and over and over again. He reads through his crate of books and then reads them again, failing to enter their pages, tumbling through lines of words only to fall back into his desolate station, with its door hinges furred with frost, nail heads bristling with ice crystals.

Not that the cold is unmanageable, not along the coast, anyway, where temperatures may rise or fall thirty degrees from one day to the next. There are dark mornings when he opens the door and the air he inhales is so frigid it makes him gasp and cough, when urine freezes before it hits the ground. But there are reprieves as well, warm enough that the sun's flattened arc brings icicles under the eaves. On these days it's almost suffocating in a bed piled with blankets. And Bigelow is spending too much time in his bed, unsatisfied lust consuming his attention as it hasn't since he was sixteen.

Somehow the Aleut woman has deprived him of his body as well as her own, leaving him numb to his own touch. He runs his hands over his chest and doesn't feel them, jerks his flesh until it produces orgasms as sudden, wet, and unmemorable as sneezes.

Perspiring under layers of wool and skins, Bigelow can't guess if the clock on the table reads nine at night or nine in the morning. Whereas masturbating used to be, like shaving or breakfast, a ritual performed once each day, providing him another means of distinguishing one dark hour from another, now it has become the opposite, a way of losing himself in time. Between orgasms he sleeps and has dreams of unrelieved tedium, plotless dreams of counting nails, winding thread on spools, chewing tasteless mouthfuls of gruel.

When the heavy sun appears, rolling sullenly along the horizon, it reveals landscapes of unutterable splendor, ice glazing every twig, turning gravel to diamonds, garbage to ransoms. On the walk down to the inlet, Bigelow holds his arm before his eyes, dazzled behind his snow glasses, treading carefully on the polished path. But what he described as grandeur in last year's letters to his mother and sister now strikes him as threatening, the inlet's water black and violent, heaving under a mantle of splintered ice.

Even if he felt like making the effort, there's nothing in walking distance that might pass for a Christmas tree. In the past year, Anchorage has consumed all the forest around itself, milled or hammered or incinerated every usable branch within miles, leaving stumps, like fields of gravestones, in the weird blue twilight of noon.

And it isn't just in winter that the light is wrong. No matter the season, the Alaskan sun is never overhead. A different incarnation entirely from the frank and workaday midwestern sun of Bigelow's childhood: Calvinist, forthright, up in the morning to show him his chores, down at night to send him to bed. A different sun from any Bigelow has known—not the inquisitive Chicago sun, beaming bright bars through the tracks of the elevated train, probing gray corners, squinting through aisles of buildings, brash, baptismal. And not the week-at-the-shore sun, heavy on the eyelids, hazy and spangled and soporific. And certainly not the cloaked, cagey sun of Seattle, never fixable in any exact spot, just a whiter patch of gray, ambient, aloof.

The Alaskan sun remains unknowable, every day a new prank, pulling along its bows and parhelia and other odd, errant optical paraphernalia, too lazy and distracted to achieve altitude, rolling along the tops of the mountains, infusing the icy fog with a strange and sullen greeny gold. Halos and sun dogs, auroral curtains of purple and pink, livid green coronas trailing ribbons of white, airborne ice devils that whirl from red to blue, secondary and even tertiary rainbows, prismatic explosions and ricocheting arcs of light, the basin of the inlet on fire, the sky dark, twinkling. From his station windows Bigelow has seen all manner of phenomena he would never before have called *weather*.

Because light bends toward the cold—toward cold's denser air—falling temperatures summon vistas that remain invisible during warmer months. Every day at noon, Mount McKinley marches south, flanked by lesser, pinker peaks, whole landscapes yanked back up over the horizon. Like sliding off the edge of the world into sleep, Bigelow thinks, only to be jerked back to the glare of consciousness.

Bigelow's breath clouds before his face, hanging still in the windless winter air. He tries to picture himself in the landscape before him. He turns, making a full circle, trying to impose an image of himself on what he sees, but he can't. The scale is wrong, or the sky, the way it presses down on the land, and its emptiness, birds as evident in their absence as when they crowded out the sun. Can a man exist here? Can Bigelow?

He hasn't mastered the required optimism. Everywhere else he's lived, he's taken his presence for granted. Here, in the north, alone now, he finds himself not quite credible.

How can it be he has no friends in Anchorage? He's not, after all, an ungenial person. He had friends in Chicago, in Seattle. University friends. Bureau friends. But, having come north alone, he finds that here he works without company, eats alone, has no money to spend in those places where men gather to talk: taverns, pool halls.

And besides not being much of a drinker or a fisher or a trapper, he's not a gambler, either, not really. The only bet he's ever made was the one on the schoolteacher, an ill-considered flirtation, and one that failed. In a town where gambling would guarantee companionship, Bigelow cannot make himself understand a bet as anything other than the invitation to throw away the few dollars he has. He believes he's not lucky; he's sure he wouldn't win.

He walks along Front Street, looking at clumps of men on corners and in doorways; they trade news about the war in Europe, usually, the loss of Russian labor, the inevitability of U.S. involvement. Sometimes he pauses in their midst; but feeling that he stops conversation, he tries to appear as casual in departure as he did in arrival.

What is it that he wants? Human contact, a person to talk to. But about what? Certainly not the weather, or his work. His work arouses suspicion in people, as if he were really only fooling the government into supporting some private crackpot pursuit. In winter, the punishments of climate seem to be of his devising. Even when his storm warnings are accurate, they seem to inspire more blame than gratitude. And on those days when his forecasts are wrong, he's the target of jokes, enough that he takes the longer, less populous route to the cable office.

He's not sure how it begins, can't remember if something sets him off, or if, as it will seem to him afterward, rage arrives like a tornado or a blizzard, a storm whose antecedents might have been plotted, had he only known what phenomena to observe. All Bigelow knows is that one moment he is standing outside the louvered shed, notebook in one hand, pen in the other, trying to turn to the current page; but there is something—a bit of food?—and the leaves of the book stick together. It's a small thing, an irritant to a person particular in record keeping, but no more than that, the kind of minuscule impediment that would ordinarily provoke a sigh, a frown. But on this day, Bigelow stamps his feet and curses, he hurls the notebook and pen at the shed, then launches himself after them. In a wild and kicking frenzy, he beats his fists and feet against the slats, splintering two, knocking others out of their frame, driving slivers into the heels of his hands, where they burn and ignite more rage. He pulls one panel off the shed, then turns on the equipment inside, shoves the thermometers over and the hygrometer, too, whacks it with his forearm and watches it fly. He tears the barometer from its stand—the instrument that only a day before he had tested with a plumb line to be sure it was standing absolutely vertical—and hurls it to the ground, watching as its tube shatters, spraying needles of glass onto the frozen mud.

The frenzy is short-lived, a minute or two, and that's it. Bigelow kneels beside the mess. The barometer, a gift from his mother and sister when he completed his training at Fort Myer, lies like something unearthed from a tomb, evidence of an earlier age of wealth and surprising refinement. He sees that even in pieces it is elegant.

He picks up the polished brass collar, uses it to push the beads of mercury together into a slippery blob. With his pen he tries to pick debris from its surface. For most Alaskans a dish of mercury suffices as a forecasting tool: when it freezes solid, stay indoors.

Improbably, all three thermometers are intact; the hygrometer, dented, will function after some tinkering. And Bigelow has another barometer, one issued by the bureau, a utilitarian instrument, its scale drawn with a mingy officiousness.

What has possessed him to destroy this thing he loves, the one object he has that partakes—partook—of other places, civilized places? Made in France, the brass collar is stamped with an address: 12, AVENUE DU CIEL, CHERBOURG. *Number 12, Avenue of the Sky.* How likely was that? Perhaps more whimsical invention than truth, and the French words inscribed on its case in fanciful, curlicued script—*Tempête, Variable, Beau, Vent, Pluie*— did make the piece more suited to a drawing room full of ladies deciding the outcome of a picnic than to a person of serious meteorological intent. Yet it was an exact instrument, and one of great charm. Each time he moved, from Fort Myer to Seattle, from Seattle to Anchorage, Bigelow packed it with care, swaddling it in layers of clothes and blankets.

At least there was no one to see his tantrum. Although,

Bigelow thinks as he picks up the broken slats, if he did not feel so alone, perhaps he would never have fallen prey to his temper.

Bits of glass and mercury gleam underfoot; too small to pick up, they elude fingers and broom straws. When he stands he's surprised by what he's seen a hundred times before: how quickly a sky can darken, on the water a few glints of silver even smaller than those underfoot.

He takes readings from his mended instruments, he enters data in his logs. He walks to and from the inlet, the creek, the telegraph office. When storms threaten, he warns the Alaska Engineering Commission, but to no purpose. Work on the railroad has ceased during these darkest, coldest days.

December. January. February. He sits at his table and chews the pads of his fingers, and the man reflected in the window's pane chews his fingers, too. The light that enters his room, that falls on his table and maps, is blue and cold. Heavy, like slabs of ice.

He tries to imagine what might have summoned her from her home. Illness? A death in her family, or a birth? Only the most dire explanations make sense to him—passages in and out of this life.

But maybe she was just tired of Anchorage, of its mud, its blocks of ugly houses, the clatter of hammers hitting ties, the seemingly inexhaustible, even rising, tide of railroad workers and prospectors, men who watched as she walked down the street.

Men who, deprived of women, reverted to animals, hands down their trouser fronts, eyes narrow, appraising. He saw what they did as she walked past; he watched, once even using his binoculars, training them on her back. She never cast her eyes down, never acknowledged the catcalls and whistles.

He lay in wait at the corner of Front and Ninth to walk with her, tried to protect her, but she wasn't having any of it. She crossed the street to avoid his company, did everything but push him away, and that, he suspects, because she wouldn't touch him in public. Instead, she returned to her house. She could wait for whatever it was she wanted.

Was that what drove her away? Not the one incident, but the assumption behind it, that she was his?

Could she have left to escape him, his relentless visits to her door, her table, her body? The thought is so painful that he closes his eyes, he shakes his head as if to refuse it.

Bigelow tries to picture the woman in places other than those few in which he's seen her—Getz's store, her chair by the stove, the bed she shared with him, the tin tub—but he can't.

Except on those nights when he wakes and sees her in his room, standing at the foot of his bed, gazing not at but through him. She looks as she did the last day he saw her, her long braid pulled over one shoulder. He knows it can't be true, her presence—in the morning, when he lights his lamp, she is gone—and yet it feels true. It feels truer than the table, the water for his coffee, the match between his cold fingers.

He scrimps on food in order to drag home another case of kerosene, pulling his sled carefully over the frozen ground. Still, the runners find a slick patch, or they catch on a stone, the sled tips, the box skids. One bottle shatters noiselessly and its golden contents leak away, leaving an iridescent trail in his wake, a prismatic oily sheen on the snow's blank face.

And when he crawls under the blankets on his bed, his dreams find another plotless monotony: he holds out his hands to catch a spilling flow, but it leaks through his fingers and is lost.

PART TWO

ACROSS THE WATER, Knik refuses to die. There's the Alaska Commercial Company trading post, a couple of roadhouses and a miners' outfitters, the Pioneer Hotel, Jenkins's Transfer and Tarpaulins, a barbershop, a saloon, and a fistful of cabins, the winter population holding at eighty-seven. When surveyors for the railroad bypassed Knik, even the postmaster quit and boarded up his office, those planks now gone, torn off by squatters. But Indians keep the town going, Indians and gold-panners and the Friday-to-Saturday dances.

May through September, a motor launch leaves Anchorage on the high tide and heads fifteen miles up the inlet's north arm, the city band on board, tuning instruments, taking requests en route. *You are my honey honey suckle, I am your bee. I'd like to sip the nectar sweet from those red lips I see.* They set up at Open Hall, just off the Pioneer's potato field: a plank floor with gaps wide enough to catch the ladies' heels as they dance, a concession offering deep-fried doughnuts, bottles of root beer, a scoop of chicken salad on a hard roll for fifteen cents.

Bigelow can't dance; he has no date. He stands in line for

chicken salad and, when it's finally his turn, surprises himself by shaking his head at the aproned girl with the big spoon. He walks off, into a clot of Indians spending their money on hooch. Bigelow puts a dime on the makeshift counter, and the transaction is accomplished without talking: a couple of ounces poured from a beaked can into a communal cup. It's clear when he holds it to the light, clear enough so dirt shows on the glass, and it has no smell. The only thing that distinguishes it from water is the way it sits in the glass, heavy with possibilities. He dips his tongue in, feels the burn. Better to get it over with—the Indians are staring—so he swallows it fast, almost fast enough to avoid coughing.

The first thing it does is dispense with shyness. Back on the dance floor, Bigelow sees a girl who might work out—why, he can't say, just a hunch based on nothing, the bracelet worn above the elbow—she won't mind, maybe, when he missteps. He cuts in, and her partner shrugs, walks off toward the outhouses. She's half and half, that much he can tell, black hair with the wrong-color eyes.

"Mika kumtux Boston wawa?" He's drunk enough to try a line in Chinook—there's something he hasn't done in a long while—asking if she understands any English. But she doesn't answer, not exactly. Something about the question, about him, is funny to her. She opens her mouth to laugh, and he sees she's missing two teeth on top, right in the front, and just like that he's hard, hard enough to want to press his groin into her hip, her side, whatever he can get away with. Strange what does it to him, nothing he could predict, and he's dancing very well, thank you. Without missing a step, he pokes his tongue into the gap, tasting the slick little absence, the incredible sweetness of her gums. He pushes until she allows her teeth to part, and they dance like that, faces pressed together, groins teasingly close, to a rollicky fast "I Didn't Raise My Boy to Be a Soldier." *No sir,*

thinks Bigelow, exempt from conscription (perhaps the only perquisite of the Weather Bureau), his mother raised him to look up at the sky, to chase clouds, count raindrops, fly kites, and jam his tongue into girls' mouths. Dancing, he discovers, is a way to get his cock harder, if that were possible.

Bootleg makes it softer, a manageable lust. Thirty cents gone, three glasses down, he's pacing himself, and he owes a word of thanks to the temperance ladies for inspiring the manufacture of illegal beverages. The night, lit by a string of bulbs, is a long one. The United States has been at war with Germany for a month, and Alaska's newly enlisted men are determined not to waste any hours on sleep before they depart for training camp. After a hundred or so turns on the floor—several times he's on hands and knees to free the girl's scuffed shoe from a crack—Bigelow gets three fingers past the girl's waistband, but after her missing teeth the pinch of flesh is a disappointment, and he goes back to kissing as he boxsteps, taking her lead. No trick to this; how is it he's never gone dancing before?

The fifth glass—he doesn't want to swallow it. Well, he does, some of him does. His brain says swallow; his throat says no. Still, who's in charge? And he's not sorry after he gets it down because this is a drunkenness that allows sublime substitutions. Bigelow finds himself dancing on the inlet, on the surface of an endless ice pan, black and almost imperceivably pitching, a degree or two with the action of the tide beneath, just enough seesaw to explain the dizzy shivers he feels as he hugs the girl in his arms, herself a sleepy, silken warm sack of compliance, sweet— she even smells syrupy, like something poured over a cake or a pudding. She tips her head to just the right angle, and, eyes closed, Bigelow follows his tongue through the gap in her smile, he slithers into the airless dark inside her, all of him: breathing, not breathing, dancing, not dancing. He won't open his eyes, he doesn't want to destroy this perfect, dangerous equilibrium; very important to keep them shut, because he's swimming inside her now, inside where it's red and claustrophobic.

But then he takes a breath, and it isn't so dire. It isn't even cramped, no, as it turns out, there's a cathedral of space inside a woman, and Bigelow, he is double-jointed, he is made for genuflection. On his knees, he hears couples glide past, the hush and scrape of shoes. How mysterious women are, like Chinese boxes, Russian dolls, except that they get bigger as you go; the one in the center is the biggest of all, her head scrapes heaven's vault. And Bigelow is holding tight to the hem of her dress, to threads unraveling:

don't let go because it's one of those bottomless plummets, the kind into which he falls some nights, legs jerking convulsively as he wakes in his bed, saving himself, saving himself from falling through himself, through her. Because that's what's happening now, he's falling through a woman's vastness: storms and oceans, a desert, a mountain, a field in bloom, the wind moving in loops and arcs and great gusting sighs, the breath of God, in out in out, God exhaling clouds of geese, and Bigelow in his tower, watching. On the bluff, over the creek, on Cook Inlet, in the territory of Alaska, vast and austere, possessing a beauty that cares nothing for the attentions of men, who crawl like ants on her face, at her feet; Bigelow watches himself drawing a map, tracing lines that only he can see, lines that give him the power to predict.

But how amazing to have found a way inside a girl that has nothing to do with fucking. Five glasses of something that looks like water, that closes the cracks in the dance floor, ices them over and lets him slide.

The launch stays the night, waiting out the ebb tide, so Bigelow comes home at sunrise, sore-footed, mosquito-bitten, puking bootleg, and considering the torment worthwhile. Here's another thing he's never done before—danced all night with a gap-toothed girl. Still young enough to keep a mental notch of experience, stuff he's collecting.

A gap-toothed, pickpocketing girl, he's forced to conclude when he doesn't have the fare back home, but still, no regrets. The captain laughs as if Bigelow's hardly the first to be fleeced in this manner. In lieu of a ticket, he accepts the promise of one dollar within an hour of disembarking.

It's not a pleasant walk to the station and back—Bigelow has to go much more briskly than he'd choose in his eviscerated condition—but Anchorage isn't big enough to allow for anonymous deceit. He returns to the muddy dock with the dollar, and then, cursing himself—how can he have been so stupid as to neglect to read his instruments?—he has to go back to the station before he can cable the bureau.

Home again, and the effort of another mile walked in the sudden heat, of straining to interpret cruelly tiny lines through a buzz of insects, brings on dry heaves and cold sweats, but still, he's not sorry. There must be a price, after all, for revelation.

For slipping inside a woman and seeing what's there.

It COMES TO HIM SUDDENLY, like a message traveling down the taut line of the kite, making it tremble with the knowledge. The Aleut left because she was pregnant.

He's sure, he *knows,* that she went off to have a child, his child. The two of them alone, away from him. But *his,* they are his.

And how far from him can they be? Not so far that their very breath doesn't, by the action of the wind, blow past, touching him.

Standing on the bluff, wind whipping tears from his eyes, he sees her navel unwind with the swelling of the flesh around it.

Then again, he thinks, back in the station house, eating under-cooked beans and washing each mouthful down with a swig of boiled creek water, this is just the kind of fantasy to which lone-liness makes a person prey.

All those hot baths afterward, her legs crossed, open, his seed leaking out.

HEARTS IN EXILE, and he's seen it twice before, he can't afford to part with another nickel; and yet there he is, one buttock tingling, the other already asleep. Ten to a bench, lice strolling from one host to the next, Bigelow leans forward, resting his elbows on his knees, hoping to keep his head out of the path of infestation. The film is projected onto an old sheet and he wonders, as he did during the previous week's showing, from whose bed the screen has been taken, from whose body flowed the now dry and ghostly stains. Not sweat, and not blood, and not urine either. Seven overlapping outlines in the center of the screen, each about the circumference of a saucer. Bigelow waits for outdoor scenes, for patches of pale sky, blank fields of snow, and, memorably, the sequence in Moscow's slum in which the heroine's white apron is sullied by the seven evocative rings: a scribbled bull's-eye hovering over her private parts.

The tent canvas flaps, the sheet wobbles, the first reel breaks twice, and the second jerks enough to make his head ache. As always, the audience is intoxicated and stands up to fight with images on the screen. Russians, Swedes, Laplanders—few read enough English to follow the title cards, but who needs plot when illusion dances so close to life? As he does once or twice a month, the Tlingit medicine man crawls in after the show has begun and goes crazy, more or less, shaking rattles and setting a handful of dried plants on fire. Threatened with a haircut once before, he is apparently going to get one this time; the cashier cuffs him to a tent pole and sends his usher to collect the barber.

But the film goes on; another reel remains; the hidden accompanist rattles her sheet music. Smoke swirls through the projector's beam, and the acrid rebuke of exorcism mingles with the moist, ripe smell of spring. Under the low canvas ceiling the air carries a complex bouquet of sweat and decay, of alcohol and unwashed hair, of swill discarded when temperatures were below zero. Whatever froze underfoot has thawed, and Bigelow gives up breathing through his mouth to avoid it, tantalized by the proximity of natives in their fish-smelling parkas. Restricted to the last three rows, they stay put, but their scent wafts forward, imparting a coy, teasingly genital savor to the dark.

Bigelow hasn't thought about it before, but when he went to a show in Seattle the music seemed to have been provided or at least suggested by whoever made the picture. The nickelodeon on King Street had an orchestra pit, and he remembers percussive battle scenes, shrill staccato chases, enchantments enhanced by harp strings. But the music in the tent theater, its human source invisible, takes little inspiration from Anna Ivanovna's odyssey through czarist Russia; instead, perhaps devised by the same tormenting intelligence that has conjured emanations of undergarments, it provides a mocking score to unsatisfied lust.

One night he saw dancing a maid so entrancing his heart caught on fire inside. . . .

No piano, no violin, and the man whose accordion wheezed through the previous week's showing isn't on hand either. There is only one voice—high and clear, innocent but not, it seems to

Bigelow, untrained, a soprano without the tremulous affect to which opera recordings have accustomed him. He turns his head to favor his ear's rather than his eye's reception. Used as Bigelow is to arias sung in languages he doesn't understand, meaning incidental to expression, he dismisses the ballad's lyrics as vulgar and tries to refocus his attention on the wobbling sheet, the heroine weeping on her knees.

"I beg you!" the title card reads, and the voice squanders another octave on nonsense.

Yip I addy I ay I ay, yip I addy I ay, I don't care what becomes of me, when you play me that sweet melody—

Just then, the film breaks again, the light goes on, Bigelow sees the singer and realizes he's seen her before. But where? She sings with her eyes closed and her face tipped up, music in her hands, but she isn't following it—she doesn't even know, perhaps, that the film has been interrupted. *Song of joy song of bliss, home was never like this. . . .*

Bigelow leans a little farther forward, his tailbone lifting off the bench. To get a better look at the girl, he asks the man in front of him if he wouldn't mind removing his hat, a Stetson whose brim hasn't bothered Bigelow during the show, and he doesn't notice that under it is the new occupant of the Aleut woman's house, the same man from whom he hid his face all winter, ducking under his parka hood on the few days warm enough to tempt everyone outside into the air.

Is she beautiful, the singer? With her eyes closed, her face betrays an abandon, even an ecstasy, that belies her smoothly buttoned bodice, the modest proportions hidden beneath its dark fabric—no operatically heaving bosom for this singer. And her skin is as luminous as if she holds all the long winter's light inside her. Her neck is long and graceful; she wears a locket on a short chain and it gleams at the base of her pale throat, resting just between the two protuberant knobs of her clavicles. She takes a breath, and as she does she inclines her head so Bigelow can see how sharp is her chin, how straight the white part in her hair, and how her dark eyebrows nearly meet over her nose.

Has he seen her before, or has she—as is his sudden impression—existed in his mind all along? The way a longing, never articulated, might find expression in a poem or a painting. An unexpectedly high, clear note.

The final note sung, the singer opens her eyes and, perhaps startled by the light and the chaotic, disheveled crowd, closes her mouth and covers it with her hand.

" 'Wait Till the Sun Shines, Nellie'!" someone yells.

" 'Good-bye, Dolly Gray'!"

" 'Pretty Baby'!"

" 'Beneath the Moon'!"

" 'You Can't Break a Broken Heart'!"

The English-speaking members of the audience—prospectors and shopkeepers, the barber who subdued the medicine man, as well as the man who lives in the Aleut woman's house—call out sentimental favorites, and the singer looks from one face to another, smiling behind her left hand, crumpling her music in her right. Her fingers, Bigelow sees, wear no rings.

"Go on, then! What are you waiting for! Christmas?" The projectionist makes a swatting gesture, loops of film spilling over his boots, and the singer bites her lip. Red blotches appear on her white throat. She drops her sheet music and bends to pick it up, swaying slowly to her feet.

Eyes closed, nodding as if to find the tempo, she embarks hesitantly on the "Battle Hymn of the Republic," chosen perhaps out of a democratic impulse, so as not to have to pick among the requests—either that or for its moral effect, an attempt to tamp down the unruly audience. She compresses her lips, drawing the first syllable out into a long, long, too long *Mmmmmmm;* but by the end of the verse the blood has drained from her neck back into her lungs, and the words swell and carry in a manner that would delight the most exacting revival preacher. The drunk Russians and Eskimos stop brawling to listen, and Bigelow forgets that he doesn't like hymns, he even forgets that once, during the second verse of this particular hymn, his mother twisted his ear painfully, pinched and held it tight to keep him from fidgeting in church.

By the time the lights are once again extinguished, the last reel jerking over the projector's sprockets, Bigelow has been shot through by so many piercing *glory*s and *hallelujah*s that he can think of nothing but holding that voice, kissing that voice, pushing his tongue farther and farther until he tastes its source.

Broke, he joins a crew digging trenches for power lines. Two dollars for a day's work, and to get there he has to take a ferry. The boat leaves in the dark, he has barely enough time to stop at the telegraph office, and then he is pitching on rough seas for an hour to arrive at a little place called Salmonberry Creek, where they're building a power station.

The job is to dig twelve feet down through what's called glacial muck, a heavy blue clay, so heavy it's like solid lead. He gets a lump of the stuff on the blade of his long-handled shovel, and it takes all his strength to heave it up onto the embankment. When he removes his gloves he finds blisters on his hands the size of dimes. He works shoulder to shoulder with Swede labor, not one of them under six feet tall and two hundred pounds. They drink Donnell's horse liniment if they can't get anything better, and the smell of it steams off their sweating backs.

After three days, Bigelow can't close his bandaged hands around the handle of the shovel, but three days is six dollars, and six dollars buys him what he needs: rice and sugar and coffee and

kerosene, and admissions to the tent theater, where he sits picking at the scabs on his palms, shifting from one numb buttock
to the other, the only member of the audience who prays for
broken reels and jammed projectors, for medicine men and
drunken brawls, for any excuse to turn the lights back on. Then
he can see the voice that spills from the slight, rapturously swaying silhouette, the voice whose shadow dances on the trembling
canvas wall. He watches her flustered hand before her mouth,
watches the red blotches on her white neck as they spread each
time from a point just above her left collarbone, watches as she
drops her music and then stoops down to pick it up. Sometimes
when her eyes are open they have the glazed cast of a sleep-
walker's; more often they dart from one to another face. She
never accustoms herself to the sight of the audience before her,
never looks at any one person long enough to allow even the
briefest transaction, never once sings a song anyone calls out to
suggest.

And after each show, when the lights come back on, already
she has disappeared, like a ghost or a sprite, a creature not quite
human. It becomes Bigelow's mission to see her as she leaves, to
learn where she goes, and by what means, but he never witnesses
her departure any more than he does her arrival, for both are accomplished in the dark. Even when he hangs about the tent flaps
after the show has begun, or slips outside before it has ended,
still he never catches her.

At home, his gramophone stands unused in a corner, the
sleeves of his records curling in the damp. He tries playing Nellie Melba singing Juliet—too sweet; then Gemma Bellincioni's
Salome—too worldly; Emmy Destinn—absolutely lifeless.
Divas, he thinks, bitterly. What did he hear in them before?
How did he tolerate such shrilly pompous sounds? He kicks at
the clumsy machine, the same that once held such power, the

staticky noises broadcast by its black horn enough to stun a group of braves. Of course, it failed him at the Aleut woman's. It didn't bewitch her. But what could have?

Walking through the town, up and down its one main street, in and out of every store: he tells himself he isn't in a hurry, he is enjoying the delicious torment of pursuit, remembering how it felt in the months—they seem a lifetime ago—when he was following the Aleut woman, catching a glimpse of her black braid in the distance.

Stalking his new, invisible quarry, Bigelow realizes that he's been dead for the past year. Dead ever since the Aleut disappeared; and while the idea frightens him—surely his essence doesn't reside with a woman, to be borne off at her whim—it's hard to regret the way he feels now that he has another focus for his longing. It's only a matter of time before he finds her in the town, during the days that grow ever longer: seventeen, eighteen, soon there will be nineteen hours of light.

But he doesn't see her, not anywhere. And no one he asks knows anything about her. No one has seen her. Oh, they've heard her, they've been to the pictures, and they nod when he asks if they remember that a singer provided auditory enhancement. But even the ones who call out song titles while the projectionist fiddles under the bulb wired to the tent pole—even they don't remember what the voice looks like, let alone where she might live.

Eᴵᴳʜᴛ ɢᴇᴀʀs of gargantuan proportion. A pulley the size of a locomotive's wheel. Bundles of rods and shafts, as well as valves, levers, springs. Cocks and caps and cranks. Innumerable bolts and bits.

It's not the elegant apparatus he imagined, and he blames this on the Aleut woman's absence. If she were in Anchorage, if he'd been able to come to her in the evenings, talk to her as he used to do, then the reel would be a different thing entirely. Streamlined and efficient.

Inspired. He would have invented it in her house, sat at her table or on her bed, sketched it in his notebook, and it would be—well, it wouldn't be this.

Hampered by what's available to him in a frontier town, he's had to bargain for parts, make do with cast-off, rusted junk. The small parts ought to be larger; the big ones are too big. He's counting on grease to keep the thing from seizing up, counting on luck, on providence.

And he's still waiting for piano wire. In the meantime he'll mount the reel outside the shed.

Bigelow lashes the apparatus onto a sledge and, on top, the gramophone, a few recordings, Caruso singing Don Giovanni, Otello. He thinks of the tenor, the one time he saw him onstage, fat and handsome, his inky, luxuriant mustache twisted up into points, the plume of his hat vibrating with what seemed like satisfaction.

Bigelow wades through dry grass on the hillside, trampling it down with his boots, pulling the sledge behind him. The runners make a hissing noise.

After playing it for her once, he'd left his gramophone at the Aleut woman's house, and it sat in a corner, unused, until she left and he reclaimed it. He is sure that even in his absence, even in privacy, she didn't listen to the recordings he brought.

Of course, his motives had not been honorable. As he walked to her house with the machine he told himself he was bringing a gift, but really he'd hoped the thing might unnerve her as it had the work crew. He saw himself comforting her, assuaging her fear with kisses. When he reached her door, he pushed it with his shoulder and it swung open; she put her arms out to take his burden from him. Her head was tilted to one side, as if in question. What strange animal did he have? Bigelow set the device on the table, unwrapped it carefully, folding the oilcloth and winding the length of twine around his hand as she sat by her stove, arms crossed.

Caruso held a note for longer than anyone might reasonably expect, and she pursed her lips in what could have been interpreted as grudging admiration, either that or boredom. With one hand on the table's edge to keep her balance, she tipped backward in her chair, and, when he came to her, she looked up. She lifted an eyebrow as if to ask whether he didn't have company enough with all those voices he'd brought with him, their keening and clamor.

Bigelow studied her face, looking for condescension, found it in her imperturbable eyes. Was she as she seemed, serenely self-sufficient, like a stone or a star, a single skin boat hurrying through the waves? He ground his face into her silence until their teeth clacked together.

On the bed, he studied her, tracing his thumb over the lines on her chin. He put a finger near one of her eyes and she blinked, but without looking at him, and when he lay above her, both of them still dressed, she struggled only if he let his weight rest too heavily on her ribs, only when he pressed the breath from her lungs.

Feeling her move under the layers of fabric that separated them, the collar of his shirt pulling uncomfortably against his neck, Bigelow was suddenly aroused. He fumbled with his own buttons, then turned his attention to hers, eager to get to her body: to armpits with their sparse straight black hairs, lines that strangely echoed those on her chin, to the shriveling dark aureoles of her nipples, the humped back of her littlest toe.

If she would punish him with her vacancy, if she would leave him alone with her body, he would trespass over all those parts she usually kept from him. He rolled her over and played with her braid. He bit at the tendons lying tight behind her knees. Slid his hand like a knife between her buttocks.

The phonograph wound down, and he left her side to crank the arm and replace the needle. Carrying the lamp back to the bed, he spread her legs to look at the dark place from which she always removed his exploring hand, the place where for months he drove himself into her. A drop of oil fell onto her smooth leg, but she didn't protest. Her face, as expressionless as her knee, betrayed nothing.

Bigelow set the lamp on the floor by the bed, and the woman's body disappeared into a well of shadow. The phonograph wound down again, but he didn't get up to crank it. Instead he remained where he was, listening to the sudden sound of rain.

After a while, the woman sat up. She swung her legs over the side of the bed and stood, walked naked to her stove. Bigelow disassembled the phonograph, removed the trumpet and latched the tone arm so it wouldn't swing, took the recording from the turntable and slipped it back into its envelope. He was hungry, so hungry that his head ached, but she wasn't cooking, she was heating water for a bath.

The two of them stepped around each other, as if each were alone in her house.

THE USUAL DISRUPTIONS get him nowhere; he has to wait for *Hell's Hinges,* the scene in which the church is burned, the drunken minister killed. Then a real riot delivers Bigelow into touching distance of the singer. It's high summer, days long enough that eight o'clock shows end like matinees, audiences dismissed into the light, blinking and disoriented. And the town is full of alcohol, railroad workers with overtime wages to spend in brothels open twenty hours a day.

Temperance and arson and firearms, Clara Williams as the minister's sister, Louise Glaum as the whore—to bleary, libidinous, overstimulated and undersatisfied eyes, a prostitute projected onto a grimy bedsheet is more than enough incentive for bench-mates to shove and curse; and on the one night that the projector doesn't catch the film on fire, a pipe-smoking prospector in the front row leans forward and does the job instead. Human conflagration follows that of celluloid. One minute Bigelow is embellishing a lurid scene with details inspired by his own romantic career; the next his nose has been bloodied by a passing elbow; and when he scrambles forward out of the way, jumping over one bench and then another and quickly ducking and turning his head to avoid further blows, a spot of his blood lands on the voice's pale blue shirtwaist, just below the swelling of her right breast.

"I'm sorry," he says.

To see where he is pointing, she puts her hand to her breast, lifts and flattens it, a gesture so pretty and awkward, so artless, that he almost falls down with desire.

"Here," he offers, and when she doesn't lift her head he says it again: "Here." He holds out his handkerchief—clean, folded, never used but carried for just such an occasion, the kind he's re-played a thousand times in his fantasies, but better, for who could conjure an explosive nosebleed?

But she doesn't take it, she pushes it away without raising her eyes.

"Go on," he says. "It's clean."

She glances at him, then looks down again; she puts her hand under his and raises the handkerchief to his bloodied face.

He is rehearsing an introduction—*I'm sorry for . . . I'm sorry to have . . .* what? *unwittingly besmirched?* No.

Perhaps he should offer to have her blouse laundered. Or is that too forward, implying as it does, taking it off? Why does she persist in staring at her feet? Shyness? Fear of blood? Should he offer to escort her outside? The projectionist steps between them, his equipment hurriedly strapped into its wheelbarrow.

"Let's go!" he says. "What're you waiting for—" But before he can add "Christmas," Bigelow takes the bloody handkerchief from his face.

"We were just leaving," he says.

The projectionist snorts. "Oh, you were," he says, and he clamps his hand on the singer's elbow and pulls her out of the tent, one hand on the wheelbarrow, the other on the silent voice, who trips along by his side, still covering the bloodstain as if she were hiding a wound.

"Wait!" Bigelow says, and the voice looks up. Her eyes meet his just long enough to offer hope.

In the station house, having run the black pennant and white square up the flagpole, indicating fair weather with temperatures higher than the preceding day, Bigelow watches through his big windows as the pole lists eastward, almost imperceivably at first, then faster, maybe five degrees in as many seconds. It doesn't hit the ground so much as recline there, his forecast spreading gently over the mud.

Impossible to dig a hole deep enough to compensate for deep midsummer thaws. Maybe he can shore it up. Water squelches up around Bigelow's boots as he walks outside. In a few days, each foot-shaped puddle will teem with mosquito larvae, tiny black fish-shaped things. The summer he arrived he collected some from a ditch, held the glass of swarming water to the light and peered through with a magnifier. Like commas or tadpoles or sperm. Except they don't so much swim as fold and unfold themselves in a furious series of jerks, ricocheting from one side of the glass to the other. A sort of irritating, itchy locomotion.

Bigelow stops scratching his bites to right the pole, first taking off the stained flags and lifting its top high enough to prop in the crotch of a spruce tree's branch. The last time this happened he managed to buttress the base with lumber, hammering wood into a clumsy approximation of what keeps church spires pointed toward heaven, then filling in the loose hole with sand and rocks and tinder. But, obviously, that hadn't worked. So now what?

Bigelow rocks back on his heels, looking at the spruce trees around him. Wind blows through their needles, a conspiratorial whisper. Here's a good idea—perfect!—he's not going to reset the pole. Instead he'll use a tree. He'll find one that's tall enough, climb up to the top, attach a pulley for the cord, climb down and cut off the limbs as he goes, then, presto: a flagpole that can't fall over!

Paregoric, he thinks as he works, sitting astride a branch and sawing the one above it. The word seems to enter his head sideways, like most thoughts of the Aleut woman. What difference if he closes his eyes, averts his gaze, busies himself with his chores? She's always there.

Tea, tobacco, toffee. Paregoric.

Why paregoric? Could it be that all along she was ill and he didn't know, hadn't cared to consider? So intent on sating the demands of his own body—his hunger, his lust—perhaps he hadn't paid sufficient attention to hers.

He shifts on the bough, and it creaks with his weight.

Well, he had paid attention, but the parts he'd scrutinized— navel, neck, armpits, the crease over her eye, or the one between her buttocks—were those that provided him purchase. They were handholds, or they were mouthfuls. They were like the little notches that climbers search out, places to insinuate fingers, toes, whatever it might take to prevent a fall.

But she'd seemed healthy enough. Strong. She could push him away with no trouble.

An addict, then. Native people were inclined to intoxicants. And paregoric is an opiate, a smooth muscle relaxant that slows peristalsis, soothes abdominal cramps, diarrhea. Bigelow knows this from his father, who suffered intestinal problems brought on by nerves. *Paregoros,* his father taught him the word. From the Greek, to console.

Was that what she had wanted? Straddling the branch, Bigelow rests his forehead against the tree's trunk, leaves the saw motionless in the half-cut bough.

He cannot think of a single instance, not one, in which he provided anything that might be considered solace.

After a hiatus of two weeks, the theater reopens, but without the voice. Bigelow endures one showing after another, barely paying attention to the pictures on the sheet. Consumed by frustrated desire, he strains through the first scenes to catch the singer's shadow as she arrives, eyes crossing with effort so that he couldn't read a title card if he tried. Then, deprived of even a glimpse of his quarry, over and over he reviews the possible contents of the locket she wears around her throat. Curl from deceased brother? Likeness of mother? Of father? Artifact of religious confirmation? Or, please no, memento of lover?

When the audience disperses, Bigelow stays behind. He asks the projectionist about the singer. "She quit," he says, latching the reel arm to the body of the projector.

"Quit? You mean for good?"

"For good?" Gnomelike, he squints up at Bigelow. "For good? For bad? I don't know. She ain't coming back, if that's what you mean."

"But—"

"Forget about her. She's . . . she ain't . . ." He doesn't finish the sentence but bends over to pick up the projector. Bigelow moves forward to help. "Don't touch it," the projectionist says.

"I only—"

"Look. She don't entertain. She don't keep company. She don't go for walks. She don't have dinner or supper or tea. She don't dance and she don't play cards. And she don't anymore go to picture shows."

"I just want to talk to her."

The projectionist laughs. "Well, she don't do that, and that's for sure."

Bigelow tries again. "Who is she? That's all I want to know."

"She ain't anybody. She used to be the picture show singer, but she ain't anymore."

"But," Bigelow says, following him out of the tent, running alongside the wheelbarrow, "I—I want to see her."

"No you don't," the projectionist says. And he says it again. "You don't."

Bigelow follows the wheelbarrow up the middle of the street, pushing after it through the roiling summer throng, people with nothing to do now that the show has let out, nothing besides drinking or gambling, and these activities aren't restricted to pool halls, not in the summer they aren't. No one stays shut behind doors when the sun is up, they sit in the street and tip their flasks and make bets on anything: heads, tails, horseshoes, cockfights, dogfights, fistfights. Whether the next woman to walk by will have her mouth open or shut, her hair up, her boots blacked. Whether she'll answer a catcall with a frown or a smile. Whether a woman will walk by at all, and how long it might take before one does.

In the midst of the sweaty crowd, Bigelow loses the projectionist. The bent man and the wheelbarrow disappear, as suddenly and mysteriously as the singer did after a show, leaving Bigelow looking around him, hands in his pockets, shaking what money he has, jingling the coins so that they make an impatient noise. Too bad he's not much of a drinker—not without the incentive of dancing, anyway—because this is a night for it, mosquitoes bedeviling anything with blood to suck, and Bigelow with money to spend, a whole fistful of unseen movies.

"Advertising for pickpockets?" The voice is familiar, and not one Bigelow associates with pleasure. He turns and sees the man with the Stetson.

"Hello," the man says. "No reason we can't be friends. After you've slept in my—" Bigelow tries to walk away, but the man holds on to his coat sleeve. "Let's take a walk," he says. "Down to the line. Stand me some refreshments and we'll call it a trade."

"Here," Bigelow says, and he holds out a handful of change. "Even?"

The man picks up the coins one by one from Bigelow's palm, counting as he does so. "Dollar . . . dollar five . . . dollar ten . . . More than a month's worth of picture shows."

Bigelow shrugs and the man replaces the coins in his hand, all except one, a dime. He holds it up. "The price of a drink," he says. "I'll accept the price of one drink."

Bigelow nods. He turns, heading back toward Front Street.

"You like picture shows," the man calls after him, but he doesn't answer. "She's Getz's daughter." Bigelow stops walking.

"Who?" he says, knowing.

"You know."

Bigelow stands for a moment, his back to the man. When he turns around to look at his face, he is gone. A hat like that—it sticks out in a crowd, but Bigelow can't see it, not anywhere.

Perhaps he's imagined the encounter, an effect of frustration, of longing. He feels in his pockets, just to see, is the money still there?

"I HAVE A THING you might like," Violet says. She offers Bigelow what looks like a dish towel, a frayed rectangle of faded blue cloth. "I know you can't stand my talking. So, here." She holds the towel out and, when he won't take it, pantomimes tying it over her mouth and around the back of her neck. "Here," she says again, and she takes a step forward, toward him. "Go ahead. We'll call it an extra. You can pay for the privilege."

It's a kind of standoff, Bigelow there in the little room, with his hands in his pockets, Violet within touching distance, one hand on her hip, the other pushing the towel at him. After a moment, he accepts it from her.

"How much?" he says, and the girl shrugs.

"I don't know. A dollar?"

He nods.

"But you won't say anything downstairs, all right? You'll give the dollar to me and not mention it?"

"Yes," Bigelow says. "All right." He remains standing as she undresses. "Everything," he says, when she stops at her chemise. Usually he lets her leave it on—even in the summer her damp room is cold—but the new agreement, the extra dollar, makes him greedy.

Or angry—maybe that's it. Angry at how transparent he must be to her, enough that she's willing to bet on it, challenge him, buy that much more of his desire. His desire that she be silent.

Silenced. He knots the towel tight. Underneath him, she makes little sticky noises as she breathes, trying to suck the saliva back into her dry throat, and the sound both provokes and arouses him. He drives her up the bed until her head bumps against the wall.

Afterward, when they're dressed, he hands her the extra dollar, but what's expensive is the look she gives him, dismissive. She's figured him out, or so she thinks; and he feels himself slide into a slot in her brain: the one who likes gags. Now, when he comes to visit her, if he does, she need not consider his case any further.

THERE'S NO REASON to hope that the gap-toothed girl is still at Knik, and anyway, Bigelow thinks as the launch approaches the dock, maybe he doesn't want to see her. She did take his money, after all.

The boat bumps against the pilings, and the captain jumps down and ties her up, heads off toward the Pioneer before the passengers have disembarked. Bigelow hangs back, then follows the crowd up the hill to Open Hall, watching a couple as they walk leaning into each other, her head on his shoulder, his hand squeezing her waist, sliding down her hip and feeling the top of her leg, then, when she apprehends it with a little slap, back up to where it began. Watching them, Bigelow feels conspicuous in his loneliness.

Perhaps he shouldn't have come. As he walks, he turns his empty pockets inside out, rehearsing the gesture he plans to make if he sees the girl. The dancers are over the crest of the hill now, out of sight, but he can hear their laughter, the occasional squawk from one of the band members' trumpets. He stops following them and stands on the path, listening as the voices grow

fainter. Around him, in the scrub, animals move—deer, rabbits—a restless tremor Bigelow feels more than he hears.

He turns around, looks behind him at the empty boat. The
tide nudges it into the dock, then lets it fall away. Having come
across the water, he's stuck here for the next ten hours. He might
as well make the best of it.

He chews his way through a sausage sandwich, so dry it
makes his eyes water, but he's no longer foolish enough to start
on an empty stomach. The Russian bootlegger has a black eye
and a split lip; his hand wavers as he pours out a dime's worth.
"Na zdorov'e," he says as Bigelow picks up the glass.

"Cheers," he tries when Bigelow doesn't answer, and Bigelow
repeats the word, "Cheers." He drains the little glass, replaces it
on the barrel head for the next customer.

Back at the dance floor, he sees the girl as soon as he steps up
onto the planks. The two missing teeth identify her, but she's
forgotten him, he can tell, and anyway the idea of showing her
his inside-out pockets seems pointless now, childish and petu-
lant. Besides, he reminds himself, it's not as if he didn't get something for the money he lost.

She's wearing new shoes, shined as shiny as patent, and he
tips his hat, he steps aside and lets her pass, watches her thighs
move under the fabric of her dress. She walks differently from
the way she dances, walks hurriedly; the strike of her heels is that
of a predator. Hearing them, Bigelow knows what he wants, to
watch her steal from other men. An endless supply of them, people like him, lonely and lusting—trusting—and she so nimble,
graceful and quick as a fish, exchanges one partner for another
without missing a beat, the lights overhead shining like moons
on the toes of her new shoes. Before the evening's over he'll have
to kiss her, push his tongue through the gap. But for now it's
enough to watch.

Was her hair the same before, coiled in that smooth figure

eight? It's not a hot night, but her pink bodice is dark at the waist, stuck wet to her skin with the effort of dancing. Mouth open, she tips her head back, aware of the effect. Whoever her partner is, even if he doesn't like the missing teeth, he has to keep looking at that place. She has a system, Bigelow sees, lets his hands go where they will, puts up just enough resistance that the man has to concentrate. After all, she wants him preoccupied as she moves in time with the music, feeling for an undone button. So fast and assured, you can't not admire her, in and out, a quick light touch, and as Bigelow sees her successes, one after another, he knows that kissing her will not be enough. Tonight he wants to fuck her.

The song is over, and she bends as if to adjust her shoe, slips a pilfered bill beneath the pale sole of her foot, making him smile because that's where he's hidden his own money, in the toe of his boot.

"I Didn't Raise My Boy to Be a Soldier." Bigelow requests the song because he wants it to be the same as it was the time before, at least in this respect. Having had another dime's worth of bootleg, he steps up to her; he places his left hand at the small of her back, feels the damp cloth, the heat of the flesh beneath. He wants to put his tongue in her mouth, but he's not going to, not yet. Whatever was in the dirty glass, it hasn't made him feel dull, just the opposite. The brass of the trumpet, the light in her eye, everything glitters sharply. Above them, stars are out, bright pricks in a black sky.

Four turns and she hasn't made a move, she's good enough at what she does that she must feel the suspicion in his body, the way he's pulled taut with attention, boxstepping a little too neatly. It isn't until he half closes his eyes and lets his head loll toward hers that her left hand drops down his side, a twitch, nothing more; he misses his chance to catch her. One pocket left, and it's a trick to be vigilant while seeming to fall asleep. She jostles him into another couple, a strategy—she's too accomplished a dancer to stumble. He shoves his hand in after hers, catches it, hot and squirming.

Bigelow drags the girl's fingers from his pocket and up to his mouth and—this isn't what he intended, he's as shocked as she—bites them, the first and the middle. Bites them hard. With a jolt she stops dancing, she snatches back the hand, wipes her fingers thoroughly on her skirt. Then she spits at him.

The scene draws an audience, amused laughter and stares. Couples dance over and stop, forming a circle around Bigelow and the girl. "Aw, Mary," someone says. "What'd he do to you?"

"Bit me," she answers, "Goddamn crazy son of a motherfucking bitch," speaking plain English and holding up the fingers, visibly dented. Several dancers lean toward her to see how the purple arcs left by his incisors interrupt the creases of her knuckles.

"I . . ." *I didn't,* he was going to say, except that obviously he had. "She's . . ." *a thief, a pickpocket.* But she hasn't taken anything from him, not this time. Bigelow feels himself sweating, suddenly drunk. A Russian the size of a walrus steps forward and grabs his shirt.

"That's my wife," he says, and he snatches up the girl's hand, holds her fingers under Bigelow's nose. "You bit my wife."

"I . . ." Bigelow tries. "Your . . ."

But what's the point? He holds his hands up in surrender. All right, he thinks, everyone gets beaten up sometime in his life. And I'm drunk, he thinks gratefully. Thank God I'm drunk.

"My—" the big Russian says.

"Shut up, Alexi!" The girl cuts him off. She twists out of his grasp, reaches up and slaps the man on the side of his head, a stinging blow that reddens his ear. She spits again, at Bigelow and at the Russian, who spits back, and then she turns on her shiny heel and walks off, dancers parting before she has a chance to shove them aside.

"Stupid," the Russian says, rubbing his ear. He stares at Bigelow, who stares back, both of them clearly wondering what's coming next.

"Buy you a drink," Bigelow tries. The Russian nods slowly, still holding the side of his head.

"*Is* she your wife?" Bigelow asks, forty cents later, the two of them sitting on stumps just beyond the dance floor, watching the girl, snug in a fat man's grasp—but not too snug, her hands are busy.

"Uh," the Russian says, nodding. "Uh-huh."

Bigelow laughs, and the Russian laughs, too.

"She make a living that way?" Bigelow asks.

"Yuh." The Russian nods, laughing hard enough now that his eyes water. Bigelow can't stop, either. His sides ache, he can hardly breathe; and the two of them go on. Gasping, they topple from the stumps.

"I . . ." Bigelow says, on the ground. He tries again. "I . . ."

"What?" the Russian says.

But Bigelow just shakes his head.

"What?"

"I danced inside . . ." He doesn't finish. *Her,* he was going to say before he realized that he couldn't make him—her husband—understand.

Lying on his back, the Russian nods gravely. "No place in Alaska," he says, "for indoor dances." And he sighs, his big chest rises and falls. "They'll build one someday," he offers, his accent thickened by drink. *Zumday.* "A ballroom."

Sobered by the idea, they lie there on their backs, silent, looking at sky between treetops.

When the band finally packs it in, the two of them are sleeping, the girl long gone, the bootlegger gone, too. All around them are bodies, faceup, facedown, snoring, hiccuping.

"Hey," someone says, nudging Bigelow with his boot, and Bigelow gets to his feet. He walks stiffly down the hill.

The boat goes back, pitching, Bigelow cold and hungry, looking for light on the water.

"Look." Getz reaches into the till and slaps two nickels down on the counter. "Here you are. The price of two shows. The price of admission to two moving pictures without accompaniment. Without the accompaniment that ain't part of the price of admission but never mind take the damn money and get the hell out. I'm sick of you." He picks the coins up and then slaps them down again, and Bigelow pushes them back.

"I don't want that," he says.

"What do you want then? What. Do. You. Want."

"I want," Bigelow says, shaking his head as if trying to dislodge what won't come out of his mouth. "I want."

Of all the men in Anchorage, of all the two thousand railroad workers, the hundreds of prospectors, the countless trappers, the mushers, the bakers, the crooked lawyers and half-trained doctors, the stevedores and the stationers, the barbers, the undertakers, the two telegraph operators, how can it be that the father of the voice is the same pinched and leering shopkeeper who watched Bigelow watch the Aleut woman? Who made, each time Bigelow came into his store for kerosene or a box of stale biscuits, a pungently salacious crack about sealskin bloomers or tattooed titties. But there you are. Getz owns the tent, he pays the projectionist, he orders the pictures and picks up the reels from the post office, and he owns the singer. He is the singer's father.

"I want," Bigelow says again.

He's been in the store three times, he's bought a peach of rude proportion, so ripe that its skin split under his lip and juice ran down his wrist and into his sleeve. He chatted solicitously with Getz as he handed him the penny, and then left without asking the question he's rehearsed. But he did talk about weather. "You heard," Bigelow said, "what happened last week? The zeppelins?" A fleet of thirteen blown off course by winds the Germans didn't anticipate, navigators blinded by fog, they were shot down over France.

Getz raised his eyebrows, daring him to continue. "There's no modern war without forecasting," Bigelow said, and he told Getz about the thirsty foot soldiers of Marcus Aurelius saved by a thunderstorm that terrorized the German tribes, securing Roman victory. About the sinking of the armada, not by the British but by storms off the coast of Scotland. Napoléon's death march across Russia. England's doomed attempt on the Dardanelles. Bigelow has a whole lecture on weather and military strategy and couldn't prevent himself from giving it to Getz.

Between visits, he walked up and down Front Street, how many times he couldn't say, too distracted to pretend an errand. And now he's come back in and can't say a thing.

"You want what?" Getz says.

"I want to know, is the, was the wom—the singer in the tent . . ."

He never uses the word *daughter,* never acknowledges what

he's checked and rechecked with other sources—barber, post-master, dentist—that the singer is in fact Getz's only child, the child of the wife that left him.

"Is she, is she coming back?"

"I told you no."

"Then is she here?"

"Here?"

"Is she here in Anchorage?"

"What for?"

"Is she—does she sing here?"

"Who wants to know?"

"Well. I do."

"In that case, no."

"But," Bigelow says, "what if it was someone else who wanted to know?"

"She still wouldn't be."

Bigelow steps away from the counter and then back toward it, like a dog trying to clear a fence. "Can I see her?" he says.

"Can you what?"

"Can I see the—can I see your . . . ?"

"See?"

"Could I talk with her?"

"She don't talk."

"What do you mean?"

"Just that. What I said. She. Don't. Talk."

"She sings."

"Yes. But that's all."

Bigelow nods. "Would you, can I ask her name?" (Because no one knows it. "She doesn't receive mail, so how would I?" the postmaster said.)

"You can ask," Getz says.

"Would you tell me it?"

Getz looks at him. "What do you want it for?"

"To know. I want to know it, that's all."

"To write her a letter?"

"Yes!" Bigelow seizes the idea.

"No."

"Listen," Bigelow tries again. "I have something for her. She might—a thing she might enjoy."

Getz smiles nastily. "What's that?" he says.

"A gramophone. And some recordings. Of singing. Opera singing."

"You want to give her a gramophone?"

"Yes. Well, no. Loan it to her."

"She has one." Getz smiles a small, triumphant, checkmate smile.

"Well, then the recordings. They're—they're quite good. You can't get them here. Caruso."

Getz snorts. "Caruso? Everyone's got Caruso."

"Well, then, Ruffo. Scotti. Eugenia Burzio."

Getz shakes his head. "Get out," he says. "I know what you're after."

THE KITE'S NOT EVEN a mile out when the reel malfunctions; the wire slips off the drum and tangles between two cogs. Bigelow sets the brake and considers the situation. It's blowing hard, twenty-five or thirty miles an hour the way it's pulling, the line angle no more than forty degrees, the kite suspended over the inlet, looking deceptively solid and terrestrial, motionless, a house built in midair. He tries stepping on the wire, just a few feet from where it comes off the reel, but it pulls out from under his boot and snaps straight up between his legs, making him jump and grab for his balls. Another inch, and that would have been that. Bigelow examines the place on his caribou work pants; the fur gone, the hide nearly cut through.

Aeolus. Favonius. Caurus. Once he knew all their names. Now he can remember only these three. The wind gods are laughing. Bigelow can hear them, gleeful and malicious.

With a double layer of gloves—rubber-lined, in case the wire has picked up atmospheric electricity—he tries to disengage the reel, but he doesn't have the strength. He can't readjust the wire on the drum without relieving the tension, and he can't pull the kite back in without getting the line back on the drum. So he'll have to cut the wire and then splice and crimp it after the reel is fixed, just what he wants to avoid, because it will never be as strong again. But what choice does he have?

His eyes watering from the wind, Bigelow tries to pull the kite in a few feet. He hangs on the wire, using gravity, his weight rather than his muscles, but the tension on the line is too high, he can't get any purchase on its slippery metal surface, and he can't wrap a loop around his gloved hand—one gust and he'd lose that hand. He'll have to attach an auxiliary line to the launch platform, through an O-ring mounted there for just this sort of mishap. Then he'll splice and crimp it to the kite wire before cutting the kite free from the reel. He turns to watch the way it sits, unmoving, in the air. The wind might slacken by nightfall, but what if it doesn't? He can't let it fly unsupervised, he can't leave the bluff until he's reeled it back in.

There are tools in the shed—a hatchet and a rasp, a hammer, spools of wire, nails, a saw and crimping pliers. Bigelow retrieves the shears and a length of wire, attaches the wire to the O-ring, and then goes to work on the kite line. To the eye, the line appears still. Even when Bigelow stares at it, he can't see what his hands feel: a singing against his palms. With all his strength, he closes the handles of the crimping pliers, willing the wires to fuse. He holds the splice, making a fist around it as he bends to cut the line free from the reel, and the vibration hums through two layers of gloves.

The new line pulls taut with an audible crack, and Bigelow winces. But the splice holds. And the O-ring is fine, made of forged steel that can withstand thousands of pounds of stress. What's wrong is the platform, the plank to which the ring is mounted. All those bent nails he hammered straight. One end comes up, and Bigelow grabs his crimping pliers to hammer it back down, but before he's finished, the other end comes up. So

Bigelow steps on it while continuing to pound the other, but what he has isn't a hammer, and the head of the pliers glances off the nails without really striking them.

Before he can figure what to do next, the plank comes free and knocks Bigelow off balance. He lunges after the board before it's out of reach. Bristling with rusted nails, it claws his cheek, his neck, but he gets one arm over it and doesn't let go, hanging on as it pulls him off the platform and onto the slope, trying to dig his heels in. But stopping is impossible; all he can do is run, ski, skid. His feet barely contact the ground; mostly he feels just a slither of dry grass and shale.

He's praying he has the strength to hold on, until, as he approaches the end of the bluff, he begins a new prayer—that he can let go, unhook himself from the nails that have worked their way right through the fabric of his tightly buttoned jacket.

Wrestling to escape his clothes, his sleeves now nailed to a board attached to a kite wire pulling him off the edge of the world, Bigelow has his head inside his collar, he can't see how many more yards—feet?—are left, when he comes to an abrupt, scratching, splintering stop. His chest thuds into what must be the trunk of one of the twisted, straggling spruce trees on the wind-whipped edge of the bluff. Whatever it is, he's got his legs around it. Coughing and gasping, the air knocked out of his lungs, he hangs on with his knees bent tight while trying to get his head and arms free.

Only minutes go by, but it seems a very long time before Bigelow has caught his breath and worked himself out of the jacket, wedged the plank securely in the crotch of the tree he hit. He's cold without the extra layer of clothing—even in summer it's windy and raw on the bluff—but he can't risk loosening the plank, so he leaves the jacket where it is, caught between the plank and the tree. He lowers himself onto the ground, sits scratched and bruised, bleeding, and, he guesses, nowhere near as sore as he'll be the next day.

The kite is still in the air, five thousand feet out, over the water, pulling so hard that the plank creaks against the tree limbs. Bigelow has to shade his eyes to see it. From his new perspective on the bluff, the kite is backlit, suddenly black instead of white, silhouetted against a lowered sun.

Bigelow waits four hours, during which every muscle stiffens, for the wind to change, lift the kite. He watches it rise overhead, then gets to his feet to reposition the plank. But as he tests the line he feels it slacken. First it isn't as taut, and then it isn't taut at all.

The kite plummets, losing altitude and looping wire all over the tree, the ground, and Bigelow, who grabs at the falling line, trying to pull fast enough to reestablish tension. But it's no good—impossible—the kite is dropping down an invisible canyon, its boxlike form warped and contorted into an aerodynamic monster, a great-beaked bird of prey bent on destroying itself.

Bigelow runs to thrust himself between the kite and what it's headed for, an outcropping of rock mottled with lichen and dusted with a few scraps of vegetation, not a shred of anything that might soften its impact. He has a moment to position himself, to squat like a wrestler, his arms out to catch or guide an edge, redirect its landing toward the slippery dry grass, then another to question his allegiance to what can't be worth more than his life: spars and fabric, instruments. And the time invested in making it, of course, the hours he spent, hundreds of them, at his drafting table. All those hours now rushing back at him.

The kite dives; Bigelow scrambles off the rocks. The kite shimmies; Bigelow squints at it from under his hands. The kite hits a low current and scoots sideways; Bigelow watches what must be an effect of wind moving over the inlet and onto land, air snaking up over the cliff, invisible and unforeseen.

Then he runs, and for a few seconds the kite and Bigelow are moving at the same speed, both of them heading back down toward the shed, Bigelow chasing, but not so fast he can't keep pace; he has that in him, anyway, a loping kind of run were he not so banged up, but, as it is, a limping run favoring his left leg, when suddenly he starts gaining on the kite. By the time he catches up to it, all he has to do is reach out, the line is there for him to take.

He has bruises all over, scrapes on his arms and on his forehead, a pulled muscle in his groin, a gash elongating one eyebrow. As for the kite—the kite remains perfect, each face white, taut, and smooth, almost smugly unblemished. Walking it back to the shed, holding its harness and yet not feeling its weight as it glides, enchanted, along puffs and whiffs of breezes, Bigelow has the sense, completely fanciful, of the kite's vanity, its amused tolerance of himself, hapless acolyte. It's been places he will never see.

In the end, after failing to devise a more sophisticated plan, Bigelow comes with his recordings to the store, where he sits on a barrel and waits. He sits on a barrel, he sits on a box, he returns to the barrel. What he wants is to sit in the sun on the front step, but he is afraid this might be interpreted as a retreat, a waning of his resolve, so he remains in the shadowy store, and Getz walks around him as if he isn't there, stepping around Bigelow's feet, standing, arms crossed, conveying his usual impatience, while Bigelow removes himself from the barrel lid when a customer requests some of whatever is swimming in the brine beneath.

Observing the storekeeper, Bigelow is impressed by the grace of Getz's performance, if performance is what it is, for the man seems not so much blind as indifferent to his presence, regarding Bigelow in much the same way as did the Aleut woman when he first followed her home, when he sat at her table and watched her chew a piece of toffee. It's only at the end of a day, when Getz closes his store, that he acknowledges Bigelow's existence, holding the door until Bigelow steps outside, then locking it behind him.

· · ·

With his recordings under his arm, Bigelow walks home in the summer light. He changes the flags on his new tree pole. He inscribes readings from his instruments into his log. He sits at his table and decodes information from the day's wireless message. He stands at his window to take advantage of the late-setting sun, tracing lines onto transparencies, and then, during the brief darkness, he lies on his bed and sleeps a seamless black and dreamless sleep.

The next day, he stops at the telegraph office en route to his vigil, stands on the sidewalk until Getz unlocks his store, then steps back inside and sits on the barrel, opera recordings stacked neatly in his lap.

For two days no customer comments on Bigelow's presence; but on the third, as if having reached an unspoken, perhaps even an unconscious, consensus, there is not one who does not.

"Who's this? Your new partner?"

"Looks like Getz has finally got himself a cat."

"Nice pickle lid."

One even sings: "When froggy came a courtin', he did ride. Uh-huh. With a somethin' somethin' and a pistol by his side. Uh-huh."

"Watch out," another warns, cryptically. "Last of her suitors didn't make out so good."

Convulsed with laughter, they fall onto the counter and Getz makes change over their heads; he smiles sourly, he ties twine around tins, he answers questions pertaining to business—no, still no mousetraps, yes, camphor on the back wall and yes, yes, a shipment of nails coming on the next boat; he retrieves items from the high shelves and spreads sawdust over spills. But he won't acknowledge that a young man sits with a lapful of music, waiting for permission to see his daughter, an invisible daughter whose name he won't reveal.

During the long days, Bigelow does not think about the singer. His mind, drugged by hours of unremitting light, skips and flits, occasionally replaying a note, or revisiting a slash of white throat, two missing teeth, three lines on an outthrust chin. A coat of feathers hanging on a nail. But without commenting on these it hurries on to other impressions, to the violet shadows that fill the ruts in the street, the flashing legs of people walking past, the pressure of his unrelieved bladder.

The year he arrived, he was insulated by the Aleut woman's flesh, for which exaggerated rhythms were natural. No matter how long or short the days, her body presented constancy—unlike Bigelow's, whose heart seems to slow during the dark months, and, when it is relentlessly bright, beats too fast. Like one of the rabbits, he thinks: at the mercy of high latitude, traveling in waves across the land, strange helpless tides of animals breaking over hills and across roads. To eat, you don't have to shoot one, just step on its neck as it washes past your boot.

He is hungry; he is thirsty, too. A June rabbit with its neck under Getz's heel, his thoughts trembling in anticipation of release.

One afternoon, captive to a manic fugue, Bigelow conceives a brilliant scheme for numerical weather prediction, a series of thermodynamical equations to be performed simultaneously around the world—computations made at 3,200 kite stations connected by telegraph and tabulated together in a kind of central ganglia, a forecast factory whose brain is set up like an orchestra pit, with a conductor waving a slide rule and members clacking abacuses. But he has no paper and pencil, and the equations flare and then die, like sparks coming off a fire: $\Delta p_G = \sin \lambda \cos \phi \, (\sin \phi)^2 \times 10^5$ dynes cm^{-2} for initial pressure distribution, and $+ \operatorname{div}(wv)$ for the increase of water per volume and per time due to convection and precipitation, $\delta M_E / \delta t =$

$- H'(\delta p_G/\delta e) + 2\omega \sin \phi \cdot M_N$ to summarize vertical velocity on a rotating globe, and for the moment neglecting quadratic terms for reasons of simplification.

Bigelow feels that the top of his head is coming off, and that he is flying through it, right out of his own brain. He is a thought, a thought of himself, combustible, an equation traveling on an updraft, glowing brightly, about to be extinguished. His arms are numb, tingling; the records slide from his lap. One, Rossini's *Otello,* shatters, and he falls off the barrel onto his knees, hearing the thunder of applause at the first kite symposium, Caruso in his plumed hat, bowing deeply at Bigelow.

"For fuck's sake, let him see the girl," someone says. The store is filled with voices.

"Let her down the stairs. You can't lock her up."

"How old is she? Thirty?"

"Who else is going to have her, I'd like to know?"

Bigelow lies on the floor, and somebody offers him a swig from a flask and, when he doesn't drink it fast enough, pinches his nose shut and tips the bottle so that its contents pour into him in a choking, smoky rush, drowning the last of his incandescent thoughts, washing away the article featuring his equations, already, in his mind, typeset in the font used by the *Monthly Weather Review.* Around Bigelow's head, legs ascend like columns into the towering, celestial realm of condensed milk and stacked tins of Postum, boxes of cornstarch, bottles of Lysol, Sapolio, cakes of P&G Naphtha, Ivory and Canthrox, Nadinola, and Snider Process pork and beans.

"Damn, but you're a mean bastard."

"I'm taking my business across to Charlie."

"Yeah, I'll spend the extra dime."

Legs shift and boots scuff, a clumsy choreography, hands reaching down trouser fronts to scratch and adjust pairs of testicles.

"Uhhhh," Getz says, a noise Bigelow has heard from livestock, the kind of huff a horse makes when someone knees its belly to tighten up the girth, and Bigelow sits up on his elbows to watch as the shopkeeper pulls his own hair.

"Miriam!" he yells. "Mirr iii aammm."

SHE LIVES WITH HER FATHER, above the store. When Bigelow pays a call on her, he has to pass Getz standing behind the counter, walk through an aisle of boxes and up eleven creaking stairs, at the top of which is a cramped windowless parlor furnished with a horsehide sofa and one ladder-back chair, a beveled mirror and a bank calendar, an upright piano with magazines and a metronome on its lid, a red wool carpet with a scorch mark on the edge near the wood stove. It's a room that requires no chaperone, as Getz can see into it from the foot of the stairs, can hear whatever conversation might occur. Behind the sofa is a door, always closed, that presumably leads to other rooms, rooms where a person might relax.

On his third visit, following one afternoon spent listening and nodding to opera, another spent looking and nodding at photographs, Bigelow brings paper and a pen.

Why won't you speak? he writes, hoping that if he, too, abandons his voice she might consent to a written exchange. But she reads the question, lifts her shoulders in an embarrassed hunch, and hands the paper back to him.

I enjoyed your singing at the shows. The pictures weren't the same without you. I stopped going. Bigelow writes what he's told her before, and she responds as she does to spoken compliments: she nods and she ducks her head, she dips her knees and plucks at the side of her skirt, all the movements together making an idiosyncratic little curtsy.

I know you can talk, he writes.

And the girl's lips twitch, she winces, she shrugs, she puts her hands to her temples and then together before her chest, and then, after this series of seemingly petitionary gestures, she shakes her head.

Confused, Bigelow smiles. *Would you rather I didn't visit you?* he asks, and she shakes her head. She takes the pen from his hand.

No, she writes, *I like your company.* Ink flows from the nib like her singing voice, a soprano kind of penmanship, Bigelow thinks, precise and pleasing, filled with points, loops, and dots.

But you won't talk to me, he writes.

She holds the pen in her hand for a long while before answering. *Not won't,* she writes, and she remains bent over the paper in her lap as if considering adding more, hunches over it for so long that he begins to worry that she is ill. But then she sits up, she hands him the page with just the two words.

"Yes, *won't,*" Bigelow says out loud. And he says it again. "Won't. You won't talk."

Miriam takes the paper and pen. *I can't,* she writes.

"But I've—I've heard you."

She nods. *Sing,* she writes on the paper.

"You sing but you don't talk?"

She points at the word *can't.*

"You sing but you can't talk?"

"She stammers," Getz says, and Bigelow looks up. The shopkeeper is standing at the top of the stairs, his hands in his pockets. His squint, his posture, the shine on his shoes, all convey not satisfaction, exactly. Vindication.

"She—" Bigelow begins.

"Stammers."

Bigelow doesn't speak but looks from one face to the other. Miriam smiles self-consciously; she tilts her head to one side and raises that shoulder: an apology. It's already occurred to Bigelow that she is unusually adept at using gesture to convey meaning; now he sees that, of necessity, she has developed a talent for it. She's wearing a white blouse with a black bow tied at the collar, the tops of its sleeves so voluminous they look empty. *Leg-o'-mutton,* Bigelow remembers such sleeves are called. "So?" he finally says.

"No," Getz says. "No. Not *so.* She stammers bad enough she can't talk."

"But I've heard—"

"You've heard her sing." Getz looks at his daughter, who sits, hands clasped between her knees, in the middle of the slippery sofa. "Show him," he says to her. "Let's get it over and done with."

Miriam shakes her head.

"Go on. Do what I say."

But she doesn't open her mouth. Her father steps into the small room, the parlor that is too small for even three people. "Say 'Hello.' Say 'How d'you do?' Say 'My name's Miriam.' Or 'Mimi,' say 'Mimi.' "

She shakes her head.

"Say, 'My name's Mimi Getz.' "

Bigelow stands between them, transfixed. The girl opens her mouth, then shuts it. She stands from the sofa and steps back, but Getz moves quickly toward her. He seizes the top of her arm, and the big sleeve collapses under his fingers so that it looks as if he's caught nothing more than a handful of fabric. "Say 'My name's—' "

"No!" Bigelow says. "Leave her. What does it matter?"

"What does it matter? Well." Getz's face is hard and assessing, the way it looks when he stands behind his counter, considering something offered in trade, a pelt or an egg. A snuffbox holding a few flakes of gold. "I'm not sure. But you'll see that it does. Matter." He shakes his daughter's arm. "Don't it, Mimi?"

The girl pulls away. She raises her chin so that the cords stand out in her white neck. Then the red blotches appear, her lips compress into a line.

"That's it," her father says, "Mmmmmm. Mmmmmy name . . ."

Bigelow watches the sinuous white neck, the jaw thrust toward the ceiling, as fine-boned as a cat's. Getz gives the arm another jerk and frees a sound, a broken *m- m- m-*, nothing more, her head tossing with the effort.

"Stop it!" Bigelow says, and Getz turns on him.

"Who are you? Who are you to tell me what to do! Is this *my* daughter? Yes! Is this *my* home? It is!" He drops the crumpled sleeve and Miriam falls back onto the couch. Like a child, she covers her face with her hands.

"Fifteen years of elocution lessons. Eight years of vocal training. Dance and rhythm and—and . . ." Getz's face is red; he swings his arms and minces his legs in parodic choreography. "Moved up here on advice of a doctor. Change of scene."

Bigelow turns away from Getz, away from his performance. "How is it you can sing?" he asks, looking at Miriam.

"You tell me!" Getz's arms go up over his head.

"What I mean is, why can't . . . ?" Bigelow looks back at Getz. "She could sing what she wants to say," he says.

"You think you're the first genius to come up with that! She can sing lyrics. She can sing nonsense. She can sing polly wolly doodle, but she can't sing a thing but what somebody else made up."

Getz drops his flailing arms and stands, staring at the girl, her face as white as his is red.

"So now you can get out. You've seen what you wanted, what you waited for. Get out and stop toying with her. She's had enough."

"But—" Bigelow says.

"But what?"

"It . . . it doesn't bother me."

"Not yet it don't." Getz looks at his daughter, who drops her eyes, then back at Bigelow. "But it will," he says. "It will."

He takes Bigelow's elbow, escorts him down the stairs and to the front door, where he pauses, his hand on the knob. "She's been married, you know. More than once." He smiles, and Bigelow sees the pleasure in this revelation.

"Not consummated the first time," Getz continues. "But the second . . . Well, that would be for you and her to"—he pauses—"talk out," he says, enjoying the irony.

Bigelow's mouth is open. Getz looks satisfied.

"But then you're a man. You've had your affairs." Getz doesn't mention the Aleut woman, but he lets go of the doorknob, he leans against the jamb and looks Bigelow up and down. With his thumbnail, he traces three lines on his chin, watching Bigelow's face to measure the effect of his gesture. "You like 'em quiet, I guess. Women that don't talk back." He studies Bigelow. "Can't say as I blame you."

When Bigelow doesn't answer, Getz sticks his tongue out, a long, narrow, nimble tongue, whose pointed end he wags in what Bigelow struggles to interpret as anything else than the universal sign for cunnilingus.

"I—" Bigelow says. "I—she—she never . . ." He stops himself before saying the words *let me*.

As it's turned out, Thursday is the day he calls on Miriam. Not that it's a formal arrangement, or even that he says to himself on a Wednesday evening that he'll see her the next day. But on Thursday, after tacking his forecast map to the wall of the post office, Bigelow stops at a bathhouse, scrubs his neck and fingernails, combs his hair with attention, and uses pomade to subdue the one persistent cowlick. On Thursday he changes his linen, he scrapes the mud from his boots, he walks to her father's store wondering how to get her to talk.

Because, much as he doesn't like to admit it, Getz is right— already he resents her pencils and notebooks. Too much of his life is devoted to written exchange, to recording data from instruments, translating it into code, exchanging his reports for more code and transcribing that. Too many attempts each day to quantify experience and fix it between the lines on a page, the outlines of a map. He's had dreams of his own penis, its shaft marked like the column of a barometer, with a scale of tiny numbers.

The weeks wear on, and as a function of human nature, Getz

grows less vigilant. Instead of hovering on the landing, he goes back downstairs; he bends over his account books; he sweeps and mops; he decants molasses from a barrel into jugs; he waits on his customers; while, upstairs, Miriam sidesteps invitations to converse or even to sing and wraps her thin arms around Bigelow, insinuates cold fingers into his pockets and sleeves and even, shockingly, down the front of his trousers. Is this evidence of passion? Shamelessness? A measure of how determined she is to avoid conversation?

Maybe she's just lonely and bored. Whatever compels her, she vacuums kisses out of his mouth with a spiraling energy, so that Bigelow, his eyes closed, actually thinks of water funneling down a drain, trying to picture what's happening, the way her lips feel as if they're munching around and around, clockwise. Once, he strangles on a laugh, imagining the two of them traveling across the equator and into the Southern hemisphere, her mouth reversing its direction. If he can pry their faces apart, all four of their cheeks shine wet with saliva, and in a half second she's back, sucking diagnostically at the muscled root of his tongue, as if trying to fathom the source of his voice.

It's astonishing how much of her mouth Miriam manages to thrust inside his, demonstrations (of affection?) so claustrophobic that he begins to pant. He feels as if he's suffocating, he can't make himself relax, his mind travels from one anxiety to another. Perhaps it would be different if he kept his eyes open, but he doesn't like seeing the room in which they sit, the bank calendar on the wall, days X'ed off one by one, the lamp by the piano, the scorched spot on the rug—discouraging, all of it. That awful horsehide sofa, the occasional glimpse of the hairs, or worse, bald spots that tormentingly evoke the animal that used to move beneath the skin. Any attempt to reconcile Miriam's kisses with the shabby domesticity of their setting is too much for Bigelow. If he leaves his eyes open, he gags on her tongue, he's distracted by a tickle of saliva on his cheek, stabbed by pins and needles in his buttock. So he closes them, he succumbs to her advances.

After, to clear his head, he walks, preferring the mud or dust of town to the solitude of a prettier destination, the invitation to measure himself against the vastness of the scenery. Across oceans, war is filling landscapes with chaos and blood, broken bodies, rubble. What is it about those X'ed-off days? He hates, *hates*, them, evoking, as they do, death. Bank calendars with their misered coins of time! The opposite of his books of maps, their lines black and defiant, infinite, marking wind and rain and fluctuations of pressure. Days without end: a book God is writing with Bigelow's hand.

He looks around himself. All the tents are gone now, and some of the log dwellings have acquired second, clapboard stories, complete with dormers and decorative cornices. A few people have picket fences, but these don't produce any civilized aspect. They look ridiculous. The town is still so new it seems a conceit, but a growing conceit. The Aleut woman's house is no longer on the outskirts; the spread of Anchorage has engulfed it. Bigelow hesitates at its bare front yard, its window like a blank, blind eye.

He snared two fox pups and ruined their skins, wasted the meat. How easy it looked in the woman's hands. He cannot understand his clumsiness. The fur seemed glued to the flesh beneath, and the newly whetted knife tore this way and that, slipping out of his grasp, biting at the muscle, the hide, the surface of the table. When he was done, the coppery fur was shot through with holes, bloodied. He dropped the first carcass and its shroud of skin in a hole, buried it, then did the same thing with the second. Except then he buried his knife next to the mutilated animal.

Did he feel it when he was with the Aleut? Did he recognize

happiness in the moment? The perfect emptiness of those evenings—each hour hanging like a pelt from her hands, each a flawless vessel—nights when he was satisfied with nothingness, a silent meal and wordless sex.

A lie. There were worries, aggravations. There must have been. But what were they? He cannot remember. All he knows is that she left him. That for weeks he came to sit on the floor of her house and stare at its emptiness.

In bed, alone, the weight of black night pressing on his eyes, Bigelow tries to redirect his lust from the Aleut woman, her chin and her armpits, her hairless smooth legs, onto Miriam. He pictures Miriam's stomach—it would be long and sinuous like her neck—and the crests of her hip bones, how they would protrude were she to lie on her back. The depth of the dip of flesh between her hips, it would be just about the thickness of his hand, were he to put it there. Never having seen Miriam without clothes, still he can imagine the whiteness of her hidden skin, its warmth, and how the fat must slip over the muscle of her stomach. Under his palm it would move just so far in one direction and so far in the other. No matter how slight the woman, always those little cushions, his favorite the plump little mound over her sex, its unruly hair and how it yields to the pressure of fingers, the halt of bone below. With Violet, he once let his teeth sink into that softness, not drawing blood, of course; she squealed, but she hadn't been hurt.

Miriam's wanton kisses suggest to Bigelow that she might let him put his mouth there, and his eye as well. In his head he can see it all and even set it to music, to verses sung by the girl herself—*your shoes ain't buttoned, gal, don't fit you right*—but his lust is not so easily reoriented. Directly, it returns to the Aleut woman, refusing to be tricked onto any other, lesser path, underscoring his enslavement to a person who has gone, left, disappeared.

Married. Married more than once. Twice?

Virginity does not have the power to enthrall Bigelow, but the vision of Getz's tongue wagging at him, the malicious, taunting pink tip of it—how could he, *how dare he,* in a conversation about his own daughter, make such a gesture?

A hundred times Bigelow has returned to the scene, attempting, if only in his mind, to respond to Getz's tongue. But it's not the kind of insult he can assuage with a remedial cleverness. By himself, during endlessly long and pacing evenings, he hasn't been able to think of anything he might have said or done to combat such, such what? Aggression? No, something worse, something more insidious. Hostility fades, but this, it's a kind of dare, a mocking, contemptuous sort of a slap whose sting increases with the passage of time.

In fact, it's Bigelow's impression that the tongue is getting bigger, even somehow longer. He goes about his chores, pursued by the tongue, never before but behind him, at about the level of his shoulder blades. Between them and out of reach, like a terrible itch, tormenting, undismissable, it chases him along the slippery mud ruts, it pokes around corners and sneaks up on him when he's working. There are only so many lines he can trace on a map before it intrudes, pink, wet, twitching.

And whenever he thinks of skipping a visit to the little room over the store, it hunts him down, it chases him up the stairs. Because, the tongue makes clear, if he lets it control his movements, if he stays away because of the tongue, then, obviously, the tongue has won.

Anticipated as a reward, each Thursday afternoon feels more like a punishment, a defeat. After an hour has passed, or two, or ten—he cannot tell the time, cannot ever contrive to get his watch before his eyes—Bigelow disentangles himself from Miriam; he smoothes her hair and her bodice, reties the undone bows and uses his handkerchief to blot her flushed and wanton face. It's alarming, the damp way she lies there on the horsehide sofa, her limbs as pliant as a hypnotist's victim. "Good-bye," he says, "I'll see you next week," provoking an intoxicated, trembling nod.

Approaching the stairs, he, too, feels shaken and confused. Sometimes his knees seem not so much to flex as to buckle when he descends. A politeness for Getz, then he reels out the door and through the streets, hurrying to the prostitute, Violet, where he has either to pay an extra dollar or listen to her blather until he jumps on her, his hand over her mouth, and rides her flesh, coming so fast it's not worth the money.

If he's to spend money on sex, it should last a few minutes, he thinks, and as an economy he's tried masturbating en route. He's stopped in the woods, crouched and furtive, adolescent, but it doesn't work. By the time he follows Violet upstairs he's hard again, and even for the second time in under an hour, it's over before it begins. What's more, no matter who he holds, in his arms or in his thoughts, by the time he comes, that woman has transformed herself. She's changed into the Aleut. Cool, detached, silent, smiling her closed-lipped smile.

Up on the bluff, Bigelow never sees the crowds he draws in town, people standing on corners, the barber with his scissors hanging from his hand, the bibbed man with his hair half cut, the waitress holding a pot of coffee, the Indians who work at the sawmill, all of them, necks cricked, watching his kite rise through the air, high above the streets and houses.

Violet and Bunch Grass and Nellie the Pig—all the girls on the Line—lean out of their windows. They run outside with hairbrushes or playing cards still in their hands, wearing nothing but camisoles and garter belts, mud squeezing up between their toes, faces lifted to the sky.

And railroad workers, too, at the end of the track, however far they've gotten that day, they stop hammering and lie on the ground, heads resting on ties. They look up to see how the silver wire catches the rays of the sun.

Now, when Bigelow walks along Front Street, people wave, they point and stare. "Today?" they ask. "Are you going to fly it today?"

The town's undertakers shake his hand, all three of them in

their black suits, plump and clean and prosperous. There's good business in high latitudes; a man in the funeral trade doesn't have to wait long for the inevitable. Something about the slant of the sun's rays, or their absence. The sheen on the rails, the relentless scream of the mill's round blade. People see gold where gold never was. They snowshoe off cliffs or into rivers. They misjudge a bear or forget to feed their dogs.

"Better than whiskey," one of the undertakers tells Bigelow, referring to the kite's white flight, an antidote to the persistently surprising weight of a filled casket.

"Thank you." Bigelow squeezes the hand too hard, unprepared for sudden popularity. "Thank you. Thank you very much."

The Chinese attendant at the bathhouse bows when he comes in.

The barber cuts his hair for free.

A boy of about eleven, pale hair and pale, serious eyes—Bigelow thinks of himself, the spring his father died—follows him from the wireless office to the dry-goods store.

"Hello," Bigelow says, but the boy doesn't answer, he runs away at the word.

Standing at the cobbler's bench, waiting in his socks while his one pair of boots are resoled, Bigelow sees a woman with a long black braid, sees her from the corner of his eye. There she is, just coming in the door, walking in behind him and reaching out to touch his sleeve. He turns, so fast he nearly loses his balance, but it's not her. It's not the woman. She.

Mɪʀɪᴀᴍ ʜᴀɴᴅs ʜɪᴍ a page torn from her notebook, a message written before he arrived.

On Monday, my father is leaving for Talkeetna's fur fair. (He's looking for extra pelts to trade at the end of the season, when the Commercial Company buyers come through.) He'll be out of town for three days at least. I have to run the store, but in the evenings I'll be free. Will you come to dinner?

Bigelow reads silently while Miriam watches. The note contains none of what Bigelow has come to regard as her conversational pauses—no crossed-out words, no blots or grammatical missteps. Looking at it, especially the use of parentheses, he's sure that she's drafted it over and over. Can see her hunched over her desk, a wet lock of hair caught between her teeth.

He opens his mouth to answer, and she puts her finger to her lips, hands him a pencil.

Yes, he writes. And then he writes, *I understand.* She takes the pencil.

Do you? she writes, and he nods.

Monday arrives, and, after posting his map, Bigelow stops by the store to watch as Miriam waits on people, using a slate and chalk for whatever words a sale requires. It's unnerving to be in Getz's General Merchandise without Getz, and Bigelow walks up and down the aisles of shelves, looking into corners, half expecting the man to jump out at him. When he hears the last customer leave, he comes up and leans on the counter. "Well," he says.

She smiles and reaches for his sleeve, uses it to pull his arm closer.

"Is it—is everything going smoothly?" he asks.

She nods, smiles, tucks loose hair behind her ears.

"Tonight?" he asks.

Tomorrow? She shrugs self-consciously and takes the slate back as soon as he's read the word. *I haven't had time to plan a meal,* she writes, adding in small cramped letters, *I want it to be good.*

"All right," he says. "Yes. Eight o'clock?"

She erases the slate with the heel of her hand. *Make sure no one sees,* she writes. *Come around through the alley.*

Getz's back entrance is cluttered with dismantled crates and leaking jars, piles of burlap sacks, flattened and dank and smelling of ammonia. Bigelow hurries past them and into the store, barely illuminated by light from the parlor above. He makes his way up the stairs, each tread creaking under his weight, making him feel conspicuous.

She's set a small table, pushed aside piano bench and horse-hide sofa to accommodate another ladder-back chair. White cloth and white candle, napkin rings, salt cellar—all these unfamiliar things, and Miriam unfamiliar, too, wearing a dress he hasn't seen before, her hair held back with ivory combs.

Spanish olives, peeled pears in thick syrup, Norwegian sardines, beans in tomato sauce, a bowl of dark cherries, the soft flesh of each puckered with an X from a pitting machine. How many cans has she pilfered from the shelves downstairs? She serves him before herself, and with his fork Bigelow tries to separate cherries from sardines, pears from tomato sauce, before they all run together.

"Well," he says, trying to sound enthusiastic. And he makes perfunctory compliments—"Pears *and* cherries!"—but, with Miriam lacking the extra hand conversation would require of her, the only answer is the sound of cutlery.

"Shall I help with the dishes?" he asks, when they've both laid down their forks. She gets up to retrieve her notebook from the top of the piano.

Leave them, she writes, and she remains standing. She pulls at his hand until he gets up, follows her through the door that's always closed during their Thursday visits, a door Bigelow has come to think of as leading into a female Bluebeard's den: photographs and used wedding bands, empty hats and shoes, suspenders hanging from pegs. But all there is, is an unadorned room filled by a big bed. At its foot there is just room enough to stand.

While he watches, Miriam undresses, the soft light from the parlor enhancing her nakedness so perfectly that she must have rehearsed the one candle's effects the previous evening. Still, he doesn't feel excited. Deceit makes him anxious, and he can't dismiss the vision of cherries overcome by fish oil.

"Mmmm?" Miriam says, kneeling on the bed. "Mmmm?" She leans forward to grasp his hand, pulls until he climbs on the mattress, unbuttons his shirt while he pulls down his trousers.

The feel of her skin against his, its ardent, adamant heat, surprises him. Here he is, he tells himself, a young man under a naked woman, and the woman has soft, deft hands, she uses both of them to rouse him. Bigelow draws a deep breath and lets it out slowly through his nose, wills himself to enjoy the attentions of Miriam, who is, if nothing else, earnest in her attentions. He's almost hard when he hears the noise of a latch downstairs.

Bigelow sits up. "Clothes!" he says. "Quick!" He looks and feels around for his trousers. Where can they be in a room so small? He slides off the mattress, gropes on the floor. The stairs begin to creak, and he gives up on the trousers and tries to claw the linens from the bed, but Miriam is sitting on them, motionless, her arms at her sides, not a heavy woman but heavy enough to prevent Bigelow from yanking a blanket out from under her.

When Getz steps into the room, dinner candle in hand, Bigelow has nothing with which to cover himself, nothing except his hands.

"Well," Getz says. "Ain't this a picture." The candle's flame leaps up, as if in shocked agreement, and Getz holds its light higher, letting it shine into every corner of the little room, showing Bigelow where his clothes have fallen, like drowned limbs clutching a raft, half on and half off the side of the mattress. To retrieve them, he has to expose his buttocks to Getz's eyes, the candle's hot flame.

"Put your clothes on, Mimi," Getz says, and Miriam slips like liquid down the foot of the bed, steps into the waiting circle of her petticoat, and pulls it up to her armpits. She's still buttoning her blue dress, buttoning it wrong, then unbuttoning and trying again, when Bigelow stands up from tying his bootlace.

Getz escorts him down the stairs with a hand squeezing his elbow, the same as he did on the afternoon he revealed that his daughter had been married before. He sets the candle on the counter and slowly, like a man unleashing an inadequately trained dog, releases Bigelow's elbow. "You'll make this right," he says. "I'm telling you now, you'll make it right."

He looks Bigelow up and down. "You think you're something in this town. Think people like you. That contraption on a string." He pulls the cash box out from under the counter, opens it as if to see whether any money is missing, as if Bigelow might be a thief as well as a seducer. "I have friends here. They'll back me up. You'll do right by my daughter." He snaps the box shut and leans forward, his face close to Bigelow's.

"She's yours now. Now that you've took her, she's yours. And you'll stand up in front of this town and say so. Say so the proper way."

THIRTY-NINE CENTS AN HOUR. The scow docks at sunup
and its captain, a rich Koniak who works for the Alaska Commercial Company, cuts the engine and just sits while his crew
unloads. Sometimes he smokes. He's all decked out in cowboy
gear—hat, leather vest, pointy boots, and incongruous chaps—
smug and fat and bad-tempered. He wears a signet ring on the
smallest finger of his right hand, and one morning Bigelow asks
to see it. YALE UNIVERSITY, it reads.

The boat is so loaded with salmon that it comes in low, scraping over the dock's gridiron, devised to prevent small craft from
sinking into the mud when the tide recedes. Larger ships can't
approach Anchorage, not yet, without a deepwater port. They
wait in the inlet, disgorging passengers and freight onto lighters
that go back and forth among the dinghies and fishing vessels,
the increasingly rare sight of natives in their skin boats.

The scow drips and stinks as the sun goes up, and the Koniak's two underlings, Indians dressed as Indians, work in an un-
characteristic frenzy; their arms almost blur as they shovel fish
out of the boat. Bigelow wonders what the cowboy might hold

over them, that they perform with such aggravated industry. The smell is sickening, but the money's not bad—maybe as compensation for the stench.

Deprived of oxygen, the fish are sluggish; they slide onto the mud bank in slimy, shining heaps, gills wide, eyes staring. A few slap convulsively against one another as they wait to be decapitated. The saddest noise, Bigelow thinks, like clumsy, drunken applause. It's his job to hatchet off their heads. Another guy takes off the fins and tails; someone else pulls out the guts. Then the last in line packs the meat into drums to be hauled off to cold storage.

The time of day, bruised and sleepy, the backdrop of mud and endless tree stumps, the adhesive scum of blood clotting underfoot, the suck of mud pulling at his heels, the fact that he never has enough money to last from one check to the next, the impossibility of his position in relation to Miriam—surely he hasn't gotten himself engaged—it all conspires to ruin Bigelow's mood. Even sunrise, splattered pink and gold over the water's dark surface, can't offset the vileness of butchering in such quantity. Still, thirty-nine cents an hour. Bigelow can make a dollar on his way home from the new wireless office, just a half mile up the bluff.

The Koniak chugs off with his crew invisible, squatting in the empty, fish-stinking hold, their lips stretched over chaws of tobacco, and then it's just the packers, however many of them show up. They divide, four or five to a line, and fall into a kind of rhythm: chop, slice, splat. Gulls stand ten and twenty deep around them, guzzling offal. They hang in the air with their beaks yawning wide, don't even have to flap if the wind's just right, unnerving, like a painted backdrop. Motionless, waiting to drop down and yank off a pink coil of intestine, sometimes fighting in midair, stretching a length of it between them until it tears or snaps, until one of them wins. Once, at the Art Institute of Chicago, Bigelow saw a painting with an angel speaking scrolls, annunciation unfurling from his lips on a pink ribbon. It disturbs him that the gulls remind him of this. The Swede who does fins is always hung over, or maybe he's sick, either with ulcers or from the work at hand; every so often he steps out of line and vomits in a curiously workaday manner, as if it meant no more to him than blowing snot from a nostril, which he also does, but without bothering to step back. Packing such quantities of fish, none of them could stomach a bite of it; they no longer think of salmon as food, they don't worry about sanitary conditions. Each of them has been issued gloves, and no one wears them.

The two or three hours pass more quickly, Bigelow discovers, if he forgoes his coffee and his breakfast. He gets out of bed in the dark, reads instruments with automatic accuracy, no higher consciousness to distract him from the simple task. He submits and collects ciphers with barely a syllable passing between himself and the telegraph operator, arrives on the dock only to slip further into a dulled stupor. The sound of the tide, the drizzle, the fog—it's as if he never got up, the rest of him sleeping while his arms go on chopping.

One morning, the Koniak shows up with a live hair seal hanging by its hindquarters, full-grown, perhaps a hundred and fifty pounds. He has it strung up over the prow, an upside-down figurehead, and Bigelow can see the weird beauty of its eyes, black and wet and shining, the fur around them stained dark. Not that he's sentimental, but it looks like weeping. The Swede makes a strangled noise, a cough of regret or disgust; or maybe he's just clearing his throat.

Bigelow doesn't want to look at the seal, but he can't help it. *"Siwash cosho mamook tumtum?"* he asks in Chinook. *What's it for?* At least he thinks that's what he says. What he means is *why,* but he's almost given up on pidgin, words that get him nowhere.

The Koniak doesn't answer. He spits on his ring and shines it on his sleeve.

"Probably got in the trap," the gutter says. He points to the load of fish, many of them mutilated, gashed, and bitten.

The seal—the way she submits—strikes Bigelow as unnatural. She doesn't look sufficiently tired to be passive. Those eyes, so mysteriously bright and black. Looking at her, he has the sense that she could escape if she tried; she could twist out of the ropes, get away from the captain with his boastful fat hands— Yale University—and be off, smart enough now to swim clear of trap leads. She won't be that hungry again.

But she just hangs there, blinking tears. Bigelow makes a move toward her. He steps forward to see her face more clearly, raises one hand, he's not sure why—was he going to touch her?—when she swings out. Her body jackknifes toward him with an ominous, keen aim, and she barks a raw, searing cough that shows him long dirty teeth, tusks almost brown at their roots, ochery and luteous and horribly superimposed on the dark red tunnel of her throat. He's shocked by the sight, the bark, the smell of her breath, fishy but somehow distinct from the stench all around him, and warm, so warm he can feel it hit his cheeks, his lips. Shocked enough to remain standing, not moving, one hand still out as if in greeting, as if, absurdly, he intended to shake her flipper.

A grotesque pendulum, the seal swings back and then returns to Bigelow, twisting and flexing her body so that her arc of travel is even farther—far enough that with one lunging thrust of her neck she seizes his raised hand in her mouth. He stands there, mute and frozen. It can't be true, but when he thinks of it later it will seem to him that even the gulls stopped their cackling shrieks; the fish were motionless, not one flapping slap or slither; the water was calm, everything so quiet that Bigelow could hear the sound of the bone in his hand as it broke.

Then the captain stands up and calls him a *peshak mesaki humm* fucking *cowmux,* or something close to it, *evil stinking dog;* the fish jump and clap in the mud, the gulls screech, the water sucks and slaps, and the Swede takes Bigelow's hatchet from his other, unbitten hand and whacks the seal neatly on the head so that she opens her mouth in surprise, she releases his broken hand.

"Fucking *cowmux,*" the Koniak says again; he shakes his head and spits.

Pain doesn't stay in Bigelow's hand; it travels through his arm and into his chest. He gasps, over and over, as if he's been punched, hard, in the breastbone. As if he's forgotten how to breathe, a sense of smothering worse than pain, worse than the nauseating warmth of blood flowing. Bigelow doesn't look at his hand; instead he stares at the seal. She shakes her head, and more blood flies around, spattering the boat and the dock, the mud, the salmon, the openmouthed packers, and Bigelow, too, standing and staring.

Her eyes are bright, and then they're not. She's dying, and he watches as it happens, holding his hand to his chest, staining his coat, his shirt. What can have transpired in that moment?

Seagulls speaking in pink scrolls. A physicist in London weighs the dying as they die; his mother sent him the article, folded as always into fourths. A delicate and exact scale that measures the weight of the soul, or so the man claimed. Bigelow can't remember the units.

The Swede raises Bigelow's hatchet again, another blow just to be sure, but Bigelow steps between him and the dead seal. "No!" he yells.

The Koniak laughs.

"No!" Bigelow yells again. "No! No!"

The Koniak reaches for a shotgun lying beside his seat. He looks capable of calm, remorseless murder, and the Swede grabs

Bigelow's elbow, incidentally moving the hand so that Bigelow doubles over.

But the Koniak isn't aiming at them. He shoots the tackle that's holding up the dead seal, blows it to bits, and the carcass falls with a heavy splat into the muck below.

It's not the Engineering Commission doctor but his assistant who sets the bone and packs the bite with germicidal powder, stitches it closed. "Better take him up to the Line," he says to the Swede, who's walked Bigelow back into town. "And buy him some liquor. He's going to need it." He hands Bigelow a roll of gauze and a packet of the germicide. "Every day," he says. "No soap or water. Keep it dry."

"Liquor?" Bigelow asks.

He shrugs. "I'd give you morphine if I had it."

Bigelow and the Swede head east along Front Street's new concrete sidewalk, twelve feet wide and eight blocks long. Neither of them speaks; the Swede still carries Bigelow's bloodied hatchet. The walk to the Line seems to take longer than usual, much longer, and storefronts look suddenly unfamiliar. Twice Bigelow stops and points with the unbandaged hand. "Was that there before?" he says.

The Swede looks where he points, at a flag snapping over the baker's sign, a pyramid of cans in the window of a dry-goods store. "Don't you live here?" he says.

Bigelow doesn't answer.

They cross a field of stumps, straggle through a stream choked with weeds, knock at the door of the house where Violet works, but it's not yet noon.

"What?" says the girl who answers. Bunch Grass or Six-Mile Mary, one of the girls whose names he doesn't like to say. Unpainted, her face looks vulnerable, lips so pale Bigelow can't tell where they leave off and the skin around them begins. It's a face like his sister's: smoothly oval, a tired crease beneath each wary eye.

"We're not open." The girl pulls what she's wearing, a faded flowery wrapper, more tightly around her body. Her bare feet are white, the flesh under the nails mauve. She catches sight of the stained hatchet and steps back.

"A bottle," says the Swede, shoving his boot in the crack before she can close the door. He points at Bigelow's bandage, a red circle seeping through. "Make it a full one."

She looks back and forth between them. "Oh all right," she says finally, and she leaves them at the door.

Expecting a wait, Bigelow sits on the step with his hand in the air, and the Swede leans against the wall. But the girl comes back promptly, wearing a fur over her dressing gown, shoes without stockings. She's brushed her hair for the transaction. "You're that fella," she says as she counts the money Bigelow gives her.

"Sorry?"

"I asked are you the one with the—" She finishes the sentence by gesturing toward the sky over the bluff.

"Oh," he says. "Yes."

And she nods, she shuts the door.

At the station, a goose lies dead on the path to his door, its neck broken. Ordinarily, Bigelow is grateful for food he doesn't have to stalk, but today the bird is a problem. How can he dress a carcass with one hand? He hangs it under the eaves and goes inside. Probably, he'll end up burying it.

A day passes, and another. Bigelow stares out his big windows, watches the wind push clouds from one frame to the next. Thoughts enter and leave his head the same way, shoved by some invisible current.

A year or so after his father died, his mother sat at her desk and tore up letters, one by one. She read them first, then held the page in her lap, staring at the wall, the same wall Bigelow stared at while doing his lessons, a faded mural of a pheasant hiding under a spray of grass. The bird looked furtive, almost frightened, as if hiding from a hunter or his dog. But, given her expression, his mother was not seeing the bird. Glancing at the letter once more, as if to be sure that she'd committed it to memory, she tore it once, twice, again, again: halves, quarters, eighths, sixteenths. She burned the pieces, and the next day, Bigelow, doing his chores, cleared their ashes from the fireplace. A few fragments still bore legible words, his father's angular hand. Bigelow squatted to read them.

Looking, it seems to him now, for a word such as *love*, or even *hate.* A word worth tearing and burning. But all he saw was *provided.*

He has a fever, and the stuff in the bottle makes it worse, but he drinks it anyway, drinks it and goes clumsily about his chores, checking instruments and making notations with his left hand, slow, careful, large numbers. Up the hill to the wireless office and home to translate the cable, drawing his map with halting, inelegant lines, and getting it to the post office by two P.M.

Too tired to take the long way home, the route that avoids Front Street, he's waylaid by Miriam, who comes running out of the store as he passes, carrying basket and notebook. *What happened?* she writes, her words hurried, less neat than usual. *We heard there was an accident down at the dock.*

In reply, Bigelow holds up his bandaged hand.

But what? she presses. *What?*

"Nothing," he says, continuing slowly up the block, Miriam following. "Hurt myself, that's all."

She pauses to write, then runs to catch up, pushes the notebook into his good hand. *I have some things for you—food. And I can help around the house. I'll come home with you and do what you say.*

"There's nothing," he says, "I don't want anything," aware that he's being ungracious, surly, and assuming she'll excuse his bad temper, blame it on what's under the bandage. Although, like an invalid or a prisoner, a creature whose temperament has been formed by dependence, Miriam possesses an uncanny ability to divine moods.

He shrugs her hand off his sleeve, and she drops back a few paces, walking behind instead of beside him. All the way to the station house, he can hear her steps, the basket brushing against her skirt as she walks.

She follows him through his door and sets the basket on his drafting table, heedless of the maps, the pens. He moves it to the floor and glowers at her, but she pays no attention, walking around, looking at the unwashed pans on the stove, the dirty plate on the table. She walks up the stairs to the room above, comes down so quickly that she can't have bothered to look out the windows.

What do you do here all day? she writes.

Bigelow sits, slumped and sighing, hand held above his head to alleviate the throb. "I'm on the bluff a lot," he answers, finally. "With the kite."

Curtains will make it much cozier, she writes in reply. *What a difference you'll see when I move in!*

She leaves him looking at the words and unpacks her basket, setting out crackers and sardines, cherries in their can.

"I'm not hungry," he says before she can reprise their terrible dinner, and she nods. She leaves the food where she set it and puts her hands together, fingers and palms aligned, a gesture of patient supplication that makes him feel both guilty and angry.

"You tricked me," he says, shoving the notebook back at her. "I want you to admit that you tricked me."

She bends over a page. *I'll change the dressing on your hand,* she writes.

"No," he says, "I'm—I want you to go home. I'm tired." He goes upstairs to avoid her face, her notebook, her welling eyes and praying hands, upstairs where he can make sure from his windows that she walks back to town. It isn't fair, he tells himself, watching as she stops and turns to look back at his station. He has no tangible reason to assume a conspiracy between Miriam and her father. Bigelow tries to see the small figure on the road as deserving of sympathy, if not love. She's passionate, anyway. If he married her he'd have sex every night, maybe sometimes in the morning. If he married her he could have sex when—well, whenever.

He takes a drink before removing the splint to change the dressing, braces himself for what's under the bandage—purple and blue and green and even black, the stitched-up bite a mere dimple in the oozing mess. The wound is infected and the hand is so fat that the sutures look like the thread restraining a mattress button. His fingers are useless, swollen shiny and stiff.

It hurts, even with bootleg it hurts, but not more than the rest of him. Oddly, he aches all over, and he keeps touching himself to check this, his arms, his thighs and shoulders and neck. Everything except his cock. He must be sick, he thinks, because he can't imagine masturbating. Instead he sits, slumped before his big windows, staring at the town, the creek bed.

Almost glimpsing a map of his own life. Invisible, or nearly so. Like wind. Like weather that he must capture and record. But how? It's so fleeting, the picture, so vast and impossible to grasp, to fix in place. Like waking from a dream: for a moment it lies before him, whole, every aspect glittering with significance. Then he leans forward, aching, stiff, and great chunks of it fall away and are lost; there's nothing, nothing to hold, nothing to keep with him.

PART THREE

SEPTEMBER. Already the train station doesn't look so raw, so new and incidental. Boots have taken the edge off the steps leading to the ticket booth. Shuffling, scuffing, stamping, Alaskans in boots, kicking against the cold. There's one now, pack on his back, breathing fog against the ticket window. He turns his head to sneeze and Bigelow recognizes the man with the Stetson, except the Stetson is gone, replaced by what looks like a helmet of fur.

Miriam, Bigelow was rehearsing silently, *Miriam, I can't marry you, I won't marry you, I'm unable to marry, unwilling to marry. I can't stand curtains or cans of sardines, I—I don't love you. Mr. Getz, I apologize for whatever advantage I may have taken, but, frankly, circumstances were misleading and unconsummated. They were . . . they were . . .* They were what?

Bigelow pats the breast of his coat, the interior pocket where he carries readings to and from the wireless office, a nervous gesture, like checking a watch fob or billfold. He flexes and straightens his fingers, testing them, a habit since the splint was removed. "Healed up all right," the doctor said, examining the hand, turning it from one side to the other. "Good thing we had that germicide. Probably never be as strong as it was. Or as limber." And Bigelow will have scars forever, even if they aren't always so purple and puckered.

"Hey," the man calls from the ticket window. "Hello!" Bigelow stops walking. "I almost paid a call on you," the man says. "I want to tell you something."

The man turns back to the window to accept change and a scrap of paper, a ticket or a receipt; he scrutinizes it, then points at something and passes it back under the pane of glass. Bigelow, still flexing and straightening his fingers, waits. It's a cold day for September, cold and unusually clear. He can see the twin masts of the wireless station, often lost in fog from this distance. Above, birds are flying—another season of dark and cold, inexorable, impossible. Every day seven minutes shorter than the one preceding. Every night seven minutes longer. How will he endure it again, then again? His breath pressed from his lungs, his soul whittled down like a soap carving.

Maybe he could marry Miriam for the winter, see how it goes. He imagines her hot skin next to his, a comfort immediately compromised by the idea of her notebook insinuating itself among his papers.

"I'm going away," the man announces, walking toward Bigelow. "I have an interest in a . . ." He stops to come up with the right word. "A concern down by Girdwood," he finishes.

"What did you want to tell me?"

"Cold by Girdwood," the man says. "What do you think of my hat?" he asks, smiling.

"Warm?" Bigelow intends a statement, but the word lilts into a question.

"Yes, it is. It is." The man smiles. He wags his eyebrows at Bigelow and the hat bumps up and down with them. He drops his pack and does a little bouncing jig on the stairs, slipping then recovering his balance. He bows deeply, and the hat stays put. "Fits snug," he says. "As you see."

Bigelow nods.

"Made for me. Custom-made. Clever seamstress, she measured my head with a string. All around." The man removes the hat, and with his finger draws a line from the center of his forehead to his temple and on around the back of his skull, then another over the top of his head from ear to ear. "Never seen a person so economical with a needle. Especially with skins. Skins are hard to sew."

The man holds the hat out to Bigelow, who reaches forward, but then, as Bigelow's fingers touch the fur, the man takes it back. "Otter," he says, and he sits down on the step next to his pack. He turns the hat in his hands. "Otter is expensive. But I didn't have to pay for this."

The sun's angled glare, the colorless cold sky, the blank silver badge of the ticket window, the gleam of tracks leading away from the town, the sound of a shovel blade against concrete, ringing brightly—all these familiar things conspire to unnerve Bigelow. He feels hairs rise on his arms, his neck.

The man squints up at Bigelow. "I was going to come to your house," he says. "I was going to pay you a visit to tell you about my hat. But then . . ."

"What?" Bigelow says when the man trails off teasingly. And he says the word again. "What?"

The needle. The fur. The accurate needle darting through the fur. He feels his heart, like an engine, turn over and catch.

"When?" he says, sitting down next to the man. "How long?" Behind them, the straight tracks shine like blades, like knives laid in the earth. The man stretches his boots out in front of him, and they both consider the sight.

"A week," the man says. "Not even."

"Is she . . . She's . . ."

"She's alone. Came back alone." The man answers the question Bigelow cannot ask. Too awful to hear any other answer. *How will I kill him?* he was already thinking of the husband, the boyfriend, whoever he might be.

From his pocket the man produces a flattened pouch of tobacco. On his thigh he rolls a small cigarette, wastes eight matches to get it lit. He holds the cigarette like a woman does, between his first and middle fingers, and Bigelow watches the smoke disappear into the colorless air.

"Thought you'd know right off," the man says, hat in one hand, cigarette in the other. "Smell her." He laughs. "I thought for sure someone would tell you. Some barber or"—he pauses—"shopkeeper. But you, I guess you don't see many people. Talk to them. You don't get out. Just back and forth to the wireless." He waves his finger up and down the empty street.

"I'm late," Bigelow says. "I'm late now." But he doesn't get up from the steps. Behind them, the ticket seller's silhouette moves on the other side of the frost-rimed glass, back and forth inside the booth, in a kind of regular rhythm. From some angles the visor is invisible, and he looks like a man, from others he is a stooped predator.

"She's . . ." Bigelow says. "She's . . ." he tries again.

"Back in the same house. Her house." The man holds the otter hat up before his face, thumbs inside the crown, fingers out. He squeezes it as if to adjust its shape, pressing the sides together, then sets it on his head.

"Why?" Bigelow swallows, ducking his head at the hat. *Mine,* he thinks. *My hat.*

"Oh, because I turned the house back over to her without any fuss. I was leaving anyway. Had my plans. Girdwood. The wind by Girdwood is intense. Run a block and your lungs freeze. Not that there is a block." He stands and Bigelow stands, too.

"What I do is, I get to Girdwood and there's a house for me.

House and job both. Job is trackwalking. Eight miles out and eight miles back, every day. Make sure it's not obstructed by anything. Snow. Tree. Carcass."

"Trackwalker," Bigelow says.

The man nods.

"I saw the notice up at the post office. Pays well."

"On account of the deaths," the man says. "For some reason, along that stretch, two walkers, one right after the other, went to sleep in the wrong spot."

Bigelow nods, trying to imagine the strangeness of such work, the loneliness to which some people were immune. Except, maybe, they weren't. Otherwise, why lie down in the wrong spot?

"So when she came back," the man continues, "I pulled my things together, and she—she didn't say, so I'm talking for her here—she had some pelts and she had a string and it took her, I don't know, less than the time it took me to pack up." He shook his head. "Two deep breaths, three—that's all it takes for them to freeze."

The man takes the ticket from his pocket, considers it, and then shows it to Bigelow. "Another two hours. Enough time to get to the Line and back for a drink."

"Oh," Bigelow says. "No. No thank you."

The man squints at him. "I wasn't talking about you," he says. "I was talking about myself."

Bigelow says nothing. He's embarrassed, but he manages to not look away.

"Lucky, your coming along just then. Well, not luck—" He laughs. "I guess I know your habits well enough to guess when you might come along. But it saves me a walk. Because I couldn't leave not knowing that you knew.

"And," he says, "I wanted to see your face."

Back from the wireless office, the first thing Bigelow does is look in the mirror. How has it changed him, this information? Is her return a secret, or is it written on him for everyone to see? The reflection stares back, his own features so strange to him that he reaches out, touches the glass.

Upstairs, in his observation room, he leans into the window facing the town, the grid of plots, the blocks of houses. To keep the binoculars from shaking, he has to prop them on an upturned box.

The house, exactly like its neighbors, is easy to find. Easy for him. Were the whole of Anchorage turned upside down, shaken, and poured out, houses tumbling like hundreds of dice from a cup, still he'd be able to find that house. Her house. He holds it in the magnified circle, watches as its black window is suddenly lit silver, like an eye opening.

A cloud has moved from before the sun.

HE RISES AT SIX to read his instruments, to fill a page of his log with numbers. Breakfast: coffee and a slice of bread sopped with molasses. He pushes aside his plate to compose the morning cable; he carries the page to the cable office, hands it to the operator even as the operator is handing him the one from Washington. "Hello," he says, or "Good morning."

"Thank you," Bigelow replies, and he carries it home.

He translates it, he makes his map, he eats his lunch, then he walks back the way he came. He hangs his map on the wall of the post office.

"Afternoon."

"Afternoon."

How is it that no one notices?

For surely he must seem vacant, perfunctory. Each day he does a hundred things without any consciousness of them. The pen in his hand moves over the page without his notice, let alone his bidding.

She. *She.*

He thinks the word over and over, a small word—three letters!—like a key turning in a lock. Inside himself he feels doors spring open.

He walks. He walks, walks, walks. Up the bluff, down the bluff. To the water's edge.

Where he finds each rock glazed with ice, the sand a flat hard expanse, black and dully gleaming, like wet macadam. Wind whips off the water, and stinging needles of ice take flight, mortifying whatever flesh is left exposed. At his feet, sea foam is frozen into patterns of overlapping waves.

Not yet winter, but cold enough that the surf is slowed and slurred by ice. Waves push in, too thick to curl, too heavy to break. Blue-white and luminous with their burden of ice crystals, they make a drunken, blurred, and hushing sound as they approach over the beach. With his clumsy thick mittens Bigclow digs stones out of the sand and drops them into the slush, testing it.

When? he asks himself.

SHE HAS A PATTERN. As surely as he comes and goes at a particular hour, so does she.

After eleven, but before noon, she comes out the door, she turns right on the street, she walks, it takes her nine minutes, to the center of town, where she does a few errands: Getz's (so Getz knows, he knows), and from Getz's several times to a building five doors up, an undertaker's and a dentist's office, and she can't keep returning to an undertaker, so it must be the dentist she visits. Bigelow peers through the office window; he lets himself in. The dentist, a mild man with spectacles, sets down the cup from which he was drinking.

"Can I help you?" he asks.

Bigelow shakes his head.

"Toothache?" The dentist stands to get to a pocket in his vest. He pulls out a watch. "I have an appointment at three, but I can take a quick look."

Bigelow stares at him. Hard to imagine her in the tilting chair, submitting to the attentions of this man with his potbelly and foot-pedal drill. Bigelow considers knocking him down, leaves before he does anything stupid.

Her teeth: small, square, and evenly spaced, except for the one lower incisor turned, perhaps as much as ten degrees out of alignment. When she let him, he'd run his tongue along the surface of her teeth, eyes closed, bumping over the one crooked one, his tongue hesitating, exploring. Mostly, though, she didn't put up with that kind of thing.

Watching her through the binoculars, he has the impression that the particular errand is of less importance than the outing itself. That she must leave and come back as a kind of ritual. For what could she need every day from town? Nothing except a glimpse of the main street, a chance to walk among the people for a moment. He remembers clearly, so clearly the first time, the finger ascending. Tea, tobacco, toffee, paregoric.

Of course, it's hard to determine much of anything from his vantage. He only knows it's the right woman because he knows the block, the house. She herself—even as revealed by a power of eighty—she is no more than a moving dot, her head indistinguishable from her torso, itself blending into her legs. Except that he can see her as if she were standing in his room before him. The three lines on her chin, the eyelashes without a curl, straight as straight. He makes her naked—and why not? She is his, this vision—the spiral navel, the hair in the fold under her arm, the breasts, smallish and pointed, the bowed legs and smooth skin. But these are for him and no one else. Back on the street, the tiny enigmatic figure travels toward Front Street, bundled beyond recognition, cloaked to all eyes but his own.

As soon as he's sure, as soon as he's watched every day for a week (assuming on those two days that he can't see through his binoculars, days of fog thick enough to obliterate the town, the houses, that she conforms to her pattern, she goes out before noon and stays out for at least an hour), he visits her house. Twelve noon exactly, and he'll stay only five minutes; he promises himself that he won't linger.

Impossible to sneak up on the place now that it's no longer on the outskirts—where is fog when he needs it? and yet it makes him nervous, the indeterminate halo it casts around the sun; he sacrifices speed for nonchalance, trying to appear as if meandering down side streets while examining an old cable receipt in his hands. But there's no one around. He darts up to the door unnecessarily fast; the hinge gives way so easily that he stumbles, he falls to his knees inside.

It will have changed, he told himself as he walked. Or the eyes that see it, they'll have changed. Someone else has lived in the house—the trackwalker—cooked in it, smoked in it, slept in it. Put his boots on the window's sill.

Bigelow has braced himself, but the room is as it was when he first walked in, when he followed her home from Getz's store. He walks around the stove, placed where it always was, the table with its two chairs. He runs his hands over the rungs of the chair on the left, his, and the other one, hers. Touches the surface of the table, that place where he was once in the habit of rubbing his thumb, a groove made by a knife or an accident of milling, a spot where the saw blade faltered. The other room, too, is as it always was, the loose cap on the bedpost that used to rattle as they moved.

All these heavy things, stove and bed and table and chairs— how has she done it? Who has helped her to transport them? Had he had his wits about him, there are many questions Bigelow might have asked the man.

He walks all around the two rooms, running his hand along the walls. It's tight; she's rechinked it so that it couldn't be tighter. And replaced the corset ad with something equally mysterious, an illustration of a clothes wringer, a smiling woman feeding a cloth into one end of the mangle.

Five minutes: they are up very quickly. He allows himself the trespass of pressing his face into her pillow, smelling it, then he goes.

HE VISITS THE HOUSE AGAIN, creeps along the road, then darts in the door, panting as he looks around the one room and then the other. Peering under a pot lid and tasting what's left in a cup. Sitting in a chair. Sitting at the table in *his* chair, a fork in one hand, a knife in the other. He knows where to find them, in the box on the shelf. Making sure, after he stands, that he has not left any trace of himself. Wiping the cutlery and putting it carefully away, then returning the chair to its exact place, a hand's width from the table.

Looking at the illustration tacked to the wall, the way the white fabric goes in one end of the mangle and then comes out squashed, the smiling woman's hand on the crank. Sitting on her bed and then smoothing it afterward, erasing his presence. Opening the door of the stove to see what's inside, embers or ashes.

Finding both house and stove cold, he clears out the ashes and lays a fire for her, first taking a handful of dry grass from the basket by the door, then picking among the kindling in the wood box, just as he used to watch her do. But then, walking away from the house, he reconsiders, quickly he retraces his steps, puts the tinder back where he found it, curses at the difficulty of regathering the ash he deposited outside the door. One errant breath of wind and it blows from his hands, scatters on the floor. He has to sweep, then, and sweep again, and sweep a third time, clumsy in his haste. He fairly runs into the town and straight to a bathhouse, where he strips behind the curtain and pays the attendant to beat the ash from his clothes while he washes it from his face and hair and hands.

BUT HE'S BACK the following day. He's in her house when he hears the noon whistle blow, probing himself for guilt, but all he finds is excitement, ascension, joy. Like the feel of kite line in his hands that first time—the tremble of connection to something alive, alive and exalted. Something flying high high above him.

He pries the lid from the tin where she keeps sweets to see: how many are there? Having checked the first time, he must do it the next, and the one after, can't not keep track of just how many she eats in a day: one. A week: seven. One each day, without exception.

Of course, he knows this about her. He knows how strict she is with regard to what she allows herself. One sweet. One pipe bowl of inexpensive tobacco. One tub of hot water, filled only enough to cover the mark, a birthmark, on her left hip. Walking around the room, hands shoved in his pockets, avoiding the window, Bigelow thinks about the woman. One carrot, a single slice of meat. One slice of bread to catch its juice. And, lying beneath him, one orgasm.

Strange, the effect on him of her restraint. He cannot quite understand it. And is *restraint* the right word? One slice, one sweet, one long, shuddering sigh: perhaps these are enough. Enough for her.

Bigelow reviews, as he has countless times, the way she unwraps a toffee, prying the silver paper up with her fingernail. While she chews, she smoothes the little square of foil on the table's surface, then, when it is flat, she folds it. When her teeth stick together, she moves her jaw from side to side to unstick them. This series of moments, each fondled in its turn like a bead on a string: it would not be inaccurate to regard it as a prayer.

THURSDAY, another Thursday that he's skipping his visit to Miriam. He'll resolve this mess—how? how?—well, somehow. But not today. A storm is gathering, and the wind is going to lift his kite that last, sixth mile it's never reached. Bigelow cables and picks up readings, raises his red and black storm flags, draws his map, and gets it to the post office early. He jogs home, sweating under his heavy parka, making a mental list of what he needs to take with him up the bluff. He'll have to hurry if he wants any light. No time for lunch. No secret visit to the woman's house. Snow glasses and water bottle and theodolite and field book and—he slams in his door, and there Miriam is, sitting at his table.

She's washed his dishes, made his bed. The place looks clean.

"Oh," Bigelow says, trying to keep hold of his list, losing items. Where's his rucksack?

Miriam hands him her notebook. *Where were you last week? And the week before? I expected you.*

"I have to take the kite out today." Bigelow sees his rucksack under the drafting table, seizes it, and begins cramming things inside.

What about me? she writes, and she holds the words in front of his face. *Thursday is my day. Our day.*

"There's a storm, and I have to fly it. I have to fly it now. I can get it up higher if the wind is right. Higher than before." He tries to move around her, but she gets underfoot, purposefully she steps in his way.

"Look!" he says.

She flips her book open to a prewritten message. *I know about the woman.*

Bigelow doesn't answer. He goes on gathering what he needs. When she grabs his arm, he shakes her off. "I'm leaving," he says. "We can talk about this later. Tomorrow."

Miriam follows him out the door, and on up the bluff. Over and over he tells her to go home, shouts at her and points, tells her that whatever her father said, whatever she thinks he owes her, is canceled out. "By perfidy!" he yells, but she ignores him. She walks resolutely in his footsteps, head down and hands hidden in the too-long sleeves of her parka, and he turns his back, hurrying, hurrying to catch the storm.

When he reaches the shed, the gusts are so strong that they snap the door open, pin it back against the wall. It's still clear, visibility for three miles at least, but wind whistles and screams over the roof as Bigelow sets the instruments and latches the hood over the module. No time to fuss with the hurricane lamp, he works in half-light, his right hand still clumsy, slow.

"Out of my way! Out of my way!" he yells at Miriam, and he pushes her into a corner. He tries to pull the kite out of the shed, but the force of the wind is too great, so he goes around behind, to the aft cell, and pushes until the front noses out of the door.

He barely has time to take out the cotter pins and release the wheels before the kite pulls out of the shed and into the sky.

Bigelow stands panting in the open door, watching as wind sucks wire out of the reel's mouth. Behind him, kneeling over her notebook, Miriam is writing.

She's not your secret. I've seen her. She's native. She's not one of us.

"You shouldn't be up here," Bigelow says. He feels in his rucksack for his snow glasses but they aren't there. Distracted by Miriam, he's forgotten them, and his water. Lucky he remembered anything. He opens his field book and notes the line angle, the wind speed, and then, leaving Miriam standing among his clutter of tools, he goes outside to sit with his back against the side of the shed. He cups his hands around his eyes to watch the kite.

He's almost managed to forget Miriam when she steps in front of him, flapping with excitement, pointing toward the reel side of the shed. Bigelow gets up and follows her, sees what she's seen. Sparks leap off the wire as if from the end of a fuse, blue, mesmerizing.

"Not grounded," he says. "The line's not grounded. I told you not to come up here."

Miriam tilts her head.

"Atmospheric electricity," he answers. "It comes down the wire."

Too late to do anything now; he doesn't dare touch any part of it, not even with insulated gloves. And anyway, as he tells Miriam, "The reel's mounted on a wood platform. Wood can't conduct electricity."

Bigelow watches the kite leap another five hundred feet into the sky and disappear, slip like a pale knife into the belly of a cloud.

"God!" he cries, reaching up. "Beautiful!" He looks at Miriam, but she's missed it. Either that or she doesn't care. He turns away, disgusted, hugging his coat closed, considering the situation he's created. One o'clock in the afternoon and dark as dusk, snow falling, except that it isn't; it's blowing parallel to the ground, stinging his face and eyes, no snow glasses, so another hour and they'll burn so badly he won't want to open them. At least the air temperature will keep the wire from getting hot enough to damage the reel, all those metal parts.

Miriam goes back into the shed and, after a few minutes, comes out with a question. *Wood keeps you absolutely safe from electricity?*

"Yes," Bigelow says. There's something in her lifted face—fear?—and he makes himself put an arm around her. Fifty-six flights without incident, data recorded and copied meticulously into his field book. He was thinking about a new page of entries as he cabled Washington and drew his forecast map, imagining what the kite might reveal as he hurried to the post office to tack up his map. If only he can get it high enough, then he can prove what he knows must be true. The air over the poles is warm—as warm as air high above the equator is cool. A great current moves between them, and Bigelow's kite will prove this. He'll get his name in all the journals; he'll be that much closer to a formula for long-range forecasting.

Miriam ducks out from under his perfunctory embrace and returns to the shelter of the shed, and Bigelow cups his hands around his eyes to watch the end of the line. Say he could change his mind and reel it back. Would he? Would he, when it seems as if he's got the whole of the sky on the end of a black, blue-sparking wire? Because that is how it looks, he can't take his watering eyes off it, gorgeous, the line tethered to the sullen clouds, a compact mass of lead gray stratocumulus of an impenetrability more ordinarily seen at lower elevations, ten or fifteen thousand feet.

But there's nothing ordinary about this day, with the wire

jerking wildly, and fire crawling down from heaven. The kite is pitching and pulling, but the kite is hidden, the kite is invisible, and on the ground it seems to Bigelow that he's contrived to work magic.

He closes his burning eyes, rests them. If everything holds, if the reel doesn't break, in an hour the kite will run out of wire and begin its automatic descent. So he'll just have to wait, squat, watch. Dizzy with hunger, he wonders what there might be to eat when he gets home. Has he gone through another sack of rice?

He thinks of the woman when he's hungry—well, he thinks of her all the time, but especially when he's hungry. Sees her sleek fingers breaking the blue-white cap of cartilage from a bone, exposing its marrow. The way she considered each morsel fastidiously before raising it to her mouth. No matter how often she did a thing, still he found it worth watching.

Bigelow lifts his head and opens his eyes.

The snow has stopped, the clouds part and then gather, revealing snatches of purple and pink, ethereal and splendid, and *high,* Bigelow thinks, *so high.* According to the reel gauge, clicking reliably, the kite is five and a half miles out. His eyes sting from the wind and snow, tears burn his cheeks with their salt.

Watching the sky, he doesn't see until after it's happened. But he hears it, a ringing noise, metal on metal, a bright violent clang that yanks him to his feet—the reel, a problem with the reel. Bigelow pushes Miriam out of the way, brushes past her hand holding his hatchet. What is she doing standing there in the wind, eyes staring wide? Why isn't she in the shed?

Bigelow knocks right into Miriam before he understands the impossible—the murderous—thing she's done, still holding the hatchet's wood handle. *Wood keeps you absolutely safe?*

The reel is stopped, and he can see where, after cutting the wire, the blade nicked a tooth off one gear.

He looks up into the sky and sees the line, sees what he thinks is the line, whisking up into the heavens.

It's gone. *Gone.* His kite, the kite he drew in his station and built on the bluff. The kite he made—like no other thing in the sky, flying alone. Untethered in a high wind, above the storm. No telling what height it will reach before it falls back to earth.

"I'll . . . I'll . . ." *kill you,* he's thinking. Bigelow lunges for Miriam, who drops the hatchet and runs.

Slipping and skipping down the frozen hillside, ice and pebbles loosened by her boots.

He lets her go.

Imagining, already, what he'll say to her father. He'll shove a finger into his chest. *Even. We're even. Official Weather Bureau instruments. Sabotaged. You have friends here? I'll cable Washington, D.C.*

Bigelow sits on the reel platform, doubles over, holding his right hand under his parka and shirt, against his bare skin. How it aches in the cold, he wouldn't have thought it possible.

TWENTY-EIGHT SPARS. 232 square feet of muslin. Five miles of piano wire at $.02 a yard. $.02 × 5 × 1760 = $176.00 = two paychecks = two months = 1440 hours' worth of piano wire. Barometer, thermometer, and dry cell battery. A hundred nights of sanding. A month of Sundays sewing. A university education. How many trips up the bluff? How many nights of insufficient sleep? How much ink, how much paper? Five miles up = 26,400 feet = Altocumulus = Cirrocumulus = Cirrostratus. Ten cents for a virgin nail, or a dollar for a hundred used ones. Thirty-nine cents an hour to hack up salmon to pay off debts. $176.00 divided by $.39 equals how many mornings of hacking, equals the loss of what? An arm? How much grief can the body withstand? Two dollars and two dollars and two more dollars for the doctor, and seventy-five cents for bootleg that doesn't stop the pain. How many hours bent over a drafting table? How many equations to determine the impact of wind speed on line curvature? First flight: September 8, 1916. Last flight: October 3, 1917. 390 days. Fifty-seven ascensions, averaging 4.3 miles, adding up to 245.1 miles. If only a person could add success to success, flight on top of flight, climbing and climbing and never coming down. No weather so high, so far from earth. No winds. No storms. 390 days is fifty-five weeks is eleven pairs of bootlaces is $5.50 spent on bootlaces alone. "Don't pull them so hard," Bigelow's mother used to say. All his life he's broken bootlaces. He has numbers in his field book— times, dates, angles, line lengths, wind speeds. He has records for the heights he reached. Thirty-one spars, if you count the three that cracked and had to be replaced. A seam every night, it took him many hours and his neck was always stiff.

There must be some calculus to apply to a loss of this proportion. But Bigelow does not know what it is.

In town, he stands outside Getz's store, considering the splintered signboard and smashed windows before going inside to look at the emptied shelves. He runs his hand over the counter, waiting for his eyes to adjust to the dim light. Someone—who?—has broken the electric bulbs overhead, dumped flour and cornmeal and something brown and sticky on the floor, scrawled over the writing on the wall, the cost of eggs, lard, kerosene. Big, black charcoal letters spell out a different word: *Pimp*.

Upstairs, the parlor has been stripped—no horsehide sofa, no piano or mirror or rug. Bigelow passes his hand under the stovepipe hanging from the ceiling to be sure, in the near dark, that the stove, too, is gone. He knocks on the metal tube and it makes a cold, echoing clang; a fine debris drizzles from its open end.

He feels his way to the bedroom door, walks through it with his arms out before him. It's cold in the room, cold and dank. The big bed is missing and Bigelow backs out quickly. He hurries through the parlor and down the stairs, spooked by a thought—ridiculous—that his rage has somehow done away with Miriam and her father. All his cursing up on the bluff has worked a spell, reduced them to nothing, the floury dust from the floor that clings to his trousers and boots.

He stamps his feet and brushes off his legs. "What happened?" he asks a man waiting next door for a haircut. With his thumb, Bigelow points over his shoulder at the ransacked store. "What happened to Getz's?"

The man squints, he wrinkles his nose as if someone has shined a bright light in his face. "Chased him out," he says.

"Who? Why?"

"Undertaker and his friends. Led a mob on the store. Getz tried to lock 'em out—they was thirty, maybe forty of them—but they busted his windows. Looted the place."

"But why?"

The man shakes his head. "Getz bragged what she'd done up the hill. Seemed proud." He shifts from one foot to the other. "You ain't the first, you know," he says to Bigelow.

"The first what?"

"Oh, the two of 'em, Getz and whatshername, Miriam, used to be they lived in Juneau." He feels in his pocket and digs out a penknife, opens and closes it before going on. "Snagged a jeweler in that town, and that jeweler had the name Baxter. Same as the undertaker on the corner of Front and Second." The man points past Bigelow. "Same because it's his brother. Engaged to be married, the whole deal, when Baxter in Juneau got cold feet and she, Miriam, took a kettle and poured boiling water on all the watches in his jewelry store. That's why Getz moved up here."

The barber, now standing in the doorway, nods.

"But where'd they go?" Bigelow asks. "Where is Getz? Miriam?"

"Police put the two of them on a train. With nothing but the clothes they was wearing."

"And the cash box," the barber says.

The man nods, looks back at Bigelow. "You wasn't—" He squints, tries again. "You didn't—" He hunches up his shoulders. "You ain't—disappointed?"

"No," Bigelow says. "I . . ." He shakes his head, doesn't bother to finish.

Bigelow buys a pound of toffee from the store down the street. "What'd they call him?" he asks the man behind the counter, wanting to hear the whole story again.

"Everything—criminal, scoundrel, extorter." The storekeeper weighs out a pound, shakes a few extra pieces into the bag. "Baxter was waiting for something like this. Him and his friends, they wanted a reason to go after Getz." He hands Bigelow the toffee. "Can you build another?" he asks.

"The instruments are gone," Bigelow tells him. "I had equipment that I sent up with it, but . . . Well, I know how to build a kite."

He puts the candy in the pocket of his coat, where it stays until the following day. Until he is standing once again in the woman's house, looking under pot lids, smoothing the fur blanket on her bed, staring at the picture of the mangle and prying open the biscuit tin where she keeps her candy. When he adds what he bought, he can hardly close the lid.

So there, he's done it. Left a message.

He walks up the street feeling strangely calm and noting that the birds overhead have thinned. The great exodus of migration is over.

Tomorrow after he goes to the cable office, he'll climb up the bluff with his binoculars. The kite has to have come down somewhere, perhaps on land, perhaps on land he can see. The image of it, spars broken, muslin caught on a branch or an outcropping, is so clear, a vision he can conjure so absolutely, that Bigelow finds himself expecting what is unlikely.

If only he can find it before heavy snows arrive and blot out its white silhouette.

W<small>HAT WILL SHE DO</small> with the candy? What will she make of it? He considers the possibilities, trying to put himself in her position. Except that she is so opaque to him, so unknowable. Even sitting across the table from her, even lying on top of her—especially lying on top of her—he never had any idea what she was thinking.

She could accept the toffees, as a kind of gift. But from whom? Will she understand that they came from him? He sees her at her table, the tin opened, the candy spilled out.

Having returned, does she think of him? He tries not to ask the more tempting question: is he, is there even a small chance that *he* is, the reason for her return?

He can't think straight, and his maps are out of focus. Not literally, for the ink comes out of the pen in its usual fashion, and perhaps a layperson wouldn't see anything amiss, but to Bigelow the work is sloppy, distracted. The correct information is there, but as if seen through a veil.

Or maybe it's just him, the veil. Maybe it's in his head. He pulls one after another of the bound volumes from his shelf, pages through them, storms and calms, looking for something. What? What can they tell him?

Cumbersome books, they weigh heavily in his lap. How hard he has labored at them, how religiously. *I made these lines,* he thinks, feeling the pages, running his hands over their surface, touching his work as he would never allow another person to do. *Day after night after day, I drew them.*

His thoughts return to the man, the trackwalker. He thinks of the eight miles between Girdwood and Bird Creek, pictures a solitary figure walking along the track, carrying a shovel, a coil of rope, whatever tools he might need to clear a drift of snow, drag a dead deer from the rails.

We do the same thing, he thinks, *I and the man.* Walking over the whiteness, inscribing a line. A line that exists independent of inscription: a track through the wilderness, a boundary drawn between one reading and another. *All we do, I and the track-walker, is make the line visible. Manifest.*

WHAT SHE DOES IS THIS: she takes them out of the tin, separating them from her own toffees, and leaves them on the shelf.

She doesn't eat them, but then neither does she throw them out.

Or docs she? Perhaps she's eaten one.

Six, seven, eight . . . Bigelow lines them up on the table, cursing himself for not having had the presence of mind to count them in the first instance, before leaving them in the tin. Thirty-one.

He replaces them on the shelf.

THE ONLY CURE, of course, is to see the woman. To stay in the house until she returns. She'll find him by the stove, waiting. With an offering of some sort. Not food, that would seem like a demand. Not soap. Not perfume. And, of course, not the gramophone. Maybe a mangle, like the one in the picture. He could get it from town. Order one. But that would take too long. A pretty plate? No, it might seem like a comment on the ones she owns. Tea, then, or tobacco.

Because he can't just come knocking on her door with a duck, not after what happened before. Because if he did, and she didn't answer, he'd—well, he couldn't stand that. So he'll have to come in and then sit. Wait.

In town, the sound of hymns. Yellow light spills from the windows of the church onto the blue snow. Sunday noon, and the frozen streets are empty. Who could see, even if they cared to, where he was going?

By noon he is at the woman's door, in her house. Because he has trespassed so thoroughly, her two rooms are as familiar to him as they were before she left, and he takes off his coat, he hangs it on the peg in the manner of a guest rather than an intruder. He arranges his gifts on the table, nothing much, just an assortment of small things—a packet of needles, a tin of cocoa, matches, and a small mirror in a hinged case. A set of two long-handled spoons.

It's warm in the house, and when he opens the stove door to check inside, he's surprised to see not just embers but flames. He sits on the chair, looking at the stabbing tongues of orange, feeding them twigs and straw from the basket of tinder. What can it mean, a fire left burning?

He could stand and go to check the back room, with its bed, the chest where she keeps the skins she traps. The shelf with the needle and the lump of beeswax. Two spools of thread: one black, one white. But for some minutes he just sits before the stove, its door open, and feeds it, single straw by single straw. Having considered the possibility that she is there, in the other room, he doesn't want to get up and look, not just yet. He's afraid of either outcome: her presence, her absence. But then, the last dry bit of grass is used. It curls into ash and drops onto the oven floor.

All along, peering through the binoculars, tracking her as she walked the blocks to the stores, visiting her house when he knew she was out, drinking from her glass, lying on her bed, all along he hasn't known what he knows in this moment: whether she is home now, in the back room, or whether she returns later, he has embarked on something irrevocable. He feels calm as he stands up from the chair. Or at least he feels resolute, aware of the awful wet pulse of his life.

He opens the door to the second room, whose only light comes from a lamp, if a lamp is burning.

She's dressed as if to go out, sitting on the bed with her hands in her lap, as still as a photograph. Wearing her dress, her only dress, with buttons all the way from throat to hem. Her hair, just exactly as it was the last time he saw her, when he watched through the window as she stared at the wall: one thick braid hangs over her right shoulder. Its end brushes her thigh.

She looks at him, neither through nor away but directly at his face in the way that she has: not surprised, not inquisitive. Not excited, not agitated. Not apprehensive. Not interested, and not uninterested, either. Not angry, not curious. Not judging. Not dismayed. Not resigned. Not amused. Not delighted, or even slightly pleased. Not displeased.

There are a hundred, no, a thousand ways that other people have looked at Bigelow over the years, and none of them describe the woman's gaze. He knows all the things that it is not. What it is, is harder to say. She has this trick of just looking.

Bigelow walks close enough to touch her but leaves his hands at his sides, and she leaves hers in her lap. After what seems a long time, she takes his right hand, the one with the scars. She turns it over, tracing the purple mark of the seal's bite, the pink shadows on his palm from blisters, kite burns. She looks up at his face, raises her eyebrows in question. He shrugs, makes a fist and unfolds his fingers, showing her how they still work.

She takes the hand back and holds it in her own, turns it over to see how the bite has gone through, scarring both sides. Then she lifts it to her mouth. Not a kiss, but the feel of her breath, warm in his hand, makes him hard. His fingers shake.

She allows him to touch her face, to cup his hand under her chin and tilt it up, to brush her cheeks with his scrubbed knuckles, smooth her eyebrows with a finger. She has no expression as he does this, but for a moment her lips part just enough that he can see a white gleam of teeth behind them. Then she closes her mouth.

He undoes the button at her throat, then the top button of his own shirt, then back to hers, one and one and one, until she gets sick of the game. At least, he thinks he sees a faint tremor of impatience at the tit-for-tat silliness of such symmetry, and she pushes his hand away and begins to undo the buttons herself. Down to her waist and then on past her lap—twenty-two buttons to keep it closed, and with each one she releases he feels himself growing that much harder, an erection that seems to claim all the blood in his body. His feet tingle; his ears ring; his head feels as light as if he's been holding his breath.

Which, he realizes, he has been. The last button slips from its hole, and he lets the air go in a rush. No drawers or petticoats, no bust bodice, no garters. Just the two pointed breasts, one nudging right, the other left, and the navel, her navel. The impossible spiral of it, like the motion of a finger turning at a temple.

Does she look satisfied as he falls to his knees? Triumphant at so complete a capture? He'll ask himself the question later. Besides, he isn't looking at her face, he's pressing his own into the warmth of her groin. Salty, and just a little rank, the unmistakable bitter tang of that smell, he's about to get his tongue just exactly where he wants it, barely enough time to begin to feel dismayed by her sudden wantonness—who has taught her this! *She,* missionary *she,* who never let him do this before!—when she twists out from under his mouth, pulls his head up by the ears.

To be sure of her constancy, if not her virtue, he tries again, and she shoves his head with both hands, hard enough to send him reeling back onto his buttocks, legs splayed, tailbone jangling with pain, so intense it kills his erection, but back it comes, revived by the relief that she is as she was, she's not putting up with anything but the straight and narrow.

Strange to be grateful for a woman who won't tolerate even the one little frill, but there he is, inside her, nose to nose, arms straight and hands off, and she with her eyes shut and fingers busy. It's insulting, so why isn't he insulted? She cries out, taking the one orgasm she allows herself, pleasure over with sooner than a foil-wrapped toffee—he hopes at least it's sweeter or deeper or what? Something. Inside her, he feels so hard, and not just his cock but hard from head to toe, blood pounding all through him, feeling better than good, better than sublime— alive, so alive!—and forget all his tricks for slowing down, he just lets himself come, biting his lip to keep from howling like an animal.

He rolls out of her way to give her room to get off the bed, to sit in her tub and scrub the smell of him off of her. But she's not in a hurry. She looks relaxed, even tired. She lies next to him, her arms still in the sleeves of her dress and her shoes still on her feet.

Bigelow looks down at what aren't the woman's old winter boots, the ones he knows. Apart from being pulled over her feet and ankles, they're not even boots. He tugs at the left one and she opens her eyes, she sits up on her elbows. There's nothing in her expression to forbid it, so he pulls the boot and it comes off in his hand—a seal flipper, unadorned, uncut, unstitched. Unlaced, because what need is there for laces? The animal's hide has been emptied of its owner, tanned and lined with dry grass, its pointed nails intact, its pearly lustrous fur smooth, the black leather marked with wrinkles too faint to feel. He touches them: soft. As soft as her own skin.

Having taken the left, he has to pull off the other, just to be sure there's a foot inside, that the pointed nails and the sleek fur aren't parts of her. But no, the foot slides out, as smooth as its mate, toes rosy and damp from the heat in the boot, a little grass caught between the smallest and its neighbor. He pulls the blade out with his teeth. The smell of them—not the usual cheesy smell of feet, but fishy. Like the sea.

Bigelow puts the boots together at the foot of the bed, side by side, gently. He buttons his shirt and the fly of his trousers, watches as she goes into the other room, pausing by the table, the gifts arranged on the surface. She smells the cocoa, opens the packet of needles, ignores the two spoons. She sets a tubful of snow on the stove.

MAKING HIS WAY HOME, Bigelow feels as if he's suffered some kind of attack, a delirium. *Perhaps I have,* he thinks, patting himself through his clothes, feeling the body beneath the coat, the muscles of his thighs as they flex to climb the hill.

He gets the chair off a man who's heading back south. Argues him down from his original price, eight dollars, without remorse. Even if it was his dead wife's favorite. Bigelow can't think about other men's problems.

The headpiece is inlaid, cherry and mahogany and other, lighter woods, oak, pine. Leaves and flowers and stars. Little iridescent circles, nacreous, made of seashells, mother-of-pearl. And tiny chips of some black stone, it must be obsidian. Bigelow runs his fingers over the design. A broad, strong seat, polished by years of use, gleaming. And strong, he tests it and it doesn't creak. The armrests finish in eloquent scrolls that match those on the crest of the headpiece. One spindle has been mended, but it's a good job, barely visible.

He points the place out to her anyway. Watches her face, a thoughtful frown. "Here," he says, pulling her to her feet. "Like this." And he sits in the chair and tips back, as far as it will go, then lifts his feet so that it rocks forward. "Now you," he says, and he stands. With his hands on her shoulders, he positions her before the chair, pushing down when she hesitates to sit. He waits for her to rock, but she doesn't, she just frowns at the chair's slight movements that echo her own.

"All right," he says, and he steps down on the front of one rocker, setting the thing in motion, her hands holding the armrests, her feet propped on the front stretcher. She lets the motion slow, then, after a moment, leans forward, pumping her head like a scaup or an eider, one of the smaller ducks, elegant with their black plumage, like the buttons on her dress. There's something funny in the movement, but he doesn't smile. He knows she can be touchy about such things.

"Look," he says. "Use your foot." He nudges her shoe with his own, but she shakes her head, preferring to keep her feet on the stretcher, as if it were a perch. Her chin goes back and forth with the effort of locomotion. Actually, he thinks, watching her, it isn't a bird she resembles. Sometimes, walking on the shore, he startles a sleeping seal, and the animal hurries toward the water, throwing her head out before her, her sleek body following. He watches the woman rock. How could he have imagined her as a bird?

A success, he thinks, pleased that he's come up with something she likes. But when it's time to go, she gets out of the tub, she follows him naked to the door.

"What?" he asks, and she points at the chair, she makes a whisking gesture with her hand as if to say, "Take it, take it back."

He shakes his head, and she shakes hers. She leads him back to the chair and picks it up by the arms, thrusts it at him.

It's the same with all the gifts: the tablecloth, the umbrella, the box of dominoes, the nutcracker. He spends his money as if he had plenty to spare. She condescends to examine what he gives her, but before they move from table to bed she replaces whatever it is in his rucksack by the door, and he ends up bringing it home to the station, the downstairs room a gallery of his failures.

Except for the box of magazines, so many months out of date that he gets them for half the cover price. A dollar for the lot of them, plus twenty cents for a box of tacks, and another dollar for a pair of lady's scissors shaped like a crane, the pointed blades coming together to make a long beak.

The woman takes them from his hand, slips her fingers through the holes. She sits on her bed as if he's not there, pages through slowly, stopping to consider each illustration. At this rate it will take her a year to get through them. And when he interrupts, when he sits beside her and points at one or another picture, she pushes his hand away, she turns aside so as to better ignore him.

"I gave you one," he says, reaching around her to lay his finger on a drawing of an umbrella. "You didn't want it." She looks at him as he puts his hand on his chest for emphasis.

"You didn't want it," he says again, but he finds he can't return her look. He can't empty his eyes of accusation, and hers— as usual they betray nothing.

He watches as she decorates the wall facing the bed: a girl with a hoop standing on a giant box of Jell-O dessert powder; an automatic Venus adjustable dress form; a woman's head emerging from a bottle of Ingram's Milkweed Cream. Once, she makes a little noise—of what? satisfaction?—as she presses the tack into the wood; then she stands back to consider her work, her face expressionless. After a minute, she takes down the dress form, replaces it with a photograph of a man and woman picnicking beside an automobile parked under a tree, but then she tears this down as well. Is there anything to be understood from the pictures she selects? The harder he thinks, the less he knows. Bigelow throws himself back on the bed, sighing loudly.

They sit across from each other, drinking tea and eating bread she has fried, slabs topped with bone butter, a substitute for the real thing made by boiling sections of antler and rendering their marrow. White and mild, it tastes good, like dairy fat. The woman finishes hers; she licks the tips of her index and middle fingers.

The table between them, the silence between them, the sheen of grease on her lips. The pucker of fabric between her third and fourth buttons. "I want . . ." Bigelow says.

She looks at him, and he stops speaking. He places his hands on the table, palms upturned.

So there's another private pleasure I've afforded her, Bigelow thinks as he walks home, grumpy, feeling his unrelieved erection, the ache in his balls, as he helplessly compares the success of the gift to her sexual excitement, orgasms to which he has trouble not attaching the word *coincidental.* The thought isn't a bitter one, not exactly. Who would she be, if she were available to him? If he could successfully insinuate himself between her gaze and its object?

IT TAKES HIM BY SURPRISE, as it did on the day he smashed his barometer. He's sitting at the table, watching as she skins a woodchuck, the animal he shot, thinking, from a distance, that it was a rabbit with its ears down. Who knows how it will taste? It's young, anyway. Its face has the blunt look of immaturity—a kind of sweet and dopey quality, it made him angry as soon as he saw it, when he stooped down, turned it over. Grass was in its mouth, and its eyes were still moist. But the sweet look and the stupidity of the creature, those remained and made him hate it. Standing over the little corpse, he considered leaving it there. But he couldn't excuse the waste.

In the chair across from his, the woman steps on its front paws to hold them firmly, while, back legs in her left hand, she uses the right to strip the hide down. Bigelow watches as the pelt turns inside out. He was hungry when he arrived, but something about the creature's feet, its long tarsals with their gummy-looking pads and dirty nails, like those of a grotesquely large squirrel, nauseates him.

The hide, when she gets it free, swings neatly from her fist, and she lays the carcass on the table to turn the skin right-side out and examine it, the density of the mud-colored fur, the surprising length of the white guard hairs. She looks thoroughly absorbed, perhaps deciding to what use she might put it; either that or its value on Front Street. How many toffees it might command.

The complete calm with which she accomplishes a task seems to mock his turbulence, his nights of agitation, of wondering how possibly to guard himself against what seems like her capriciousness, another unexplained disappearance. *She will leave. She will leave. She will leave.* He's made the three words into a refrain, sung them over and over as a kind of defensive training. But how laughable. How pathetic and useless an exercise.

Abruptly, Bigelow is jolted into a wild temper. He jumps up from his chair so suddenly that she looks from him to the stove, as if assuming he's been burned, a cinder must have flown out of the open door.

In a minute he's on her, he's pulled the oily-feeling pelt from her hands and thrown it across the room, picked up the naked animal and dashed it on the table so that its head makes a dull thud.

"I hate you!" he says, yelling the words. "Stupid! You're no better than a dog the way you sit there!" He flails at her, without actually making contact, and she steps out of reach.

"Come back at me!" he cries. "Why don't you!" He lunges forward, grabs her shoulders to shake them, and she eludes him with a neat swift twist, so that he's left with empty hands; and she, standing some distance away, regards him impassively, as if she's seen things he can't imagine. What could he do that might surprise her?

Nothing, judging from her calm regard, and yet this doesn't stop him from wrecking the house as she watches. He turns over the table and chairs, stomps on one so that he breaks its back leg, splinters a stretcher. At this she looks pained, but it's a kind of look reserved for spills, for wear and tear—she's not threatened. Not by that or by his hurling everything he can get hands on, parkas and boots and cups, ladles, broom and dustpan, box of toffees, canister of tea. Tobacco and pipe and tub and towel. The kettle and the frying pan.

Throughout, the woman stands to the side, avoiding his touch. It's as if he's nothing, nothing personal. Like wind or water, like the weather itself, soon he'll be spent, he'll have worn himself out and she'll right the furniture, she'll go on with her chores. A man, that's all he is, the outline of his psyche like that of his cock, one minute all puffed up hard, bellicose, the next spent and shriveled.

Bigelow falls facedown into the furs that he's pulled off the bed and, inside himself, keeps falling. Down and down, into wracking seizures of sobs. The more it seems that words are useless, the more of them he uses, while she sits silent on the stripped bed.

"What do you think! That you can just leave, just like that! No warning! No explanation! I came here. You were gone. I came back. Every day. I was here every day! I waited. I waited because I didn't believe that you would just go. Disappear without telling me somehow."

He has to force himself to lift his face out of the fur, to look at her sitting on the stripped bed, bits of straw poking through the mattress ticking. He wants to put his head in her lap, but there's nothing in her posture, her crossed arms and set lips, to indicate she'd allow any such gesture, so he stands. He begins to clean up.

By chance, there's a piece of kindling that's straight and the same length as the splintered stretcher. All he has to do is peel off the bark and whittle the ends so that it fits. She sits on the bed, arms still crossed, watching as he works. Under her gaze, he picks up the mended chair and sits carefully, testing it. He puts the furniture back where it belongs, table before the stove, and he replaces objects on the shelf.

All right, he thinks as he works. *All right.*

And, like someone reciting a prayer, he goes over the remainder of the afternoon. *She will cook and we will eat. We'll sit across from each other without saying a thing, and when we're finished, we'll get into the bed. And she'll touch herself. She'll reach down when I'm inside her and make herself cry out—the first little noise from her after all that I've made. I'll come, and then maybe she'll let me hold her, but probably not. She'll take a bath, and I'll sleep. I'll sleep a little before going back to the station. And tomorrow, tomorrow I'll wake up in my bed. For a minute I'll lie there, and then I'll go outside to the instruments and write the numbers in the log and transcribe them into code and carry the page to the cable office. And come home. I'll come home every day to draw my maps, the maps for me, for the book of storm tracks, and the forecast maps for the post office. There will be time left over, some afternoons, to build a new kite. Muslin is cheap, and wood for the spars. I know the dimensions. No instruments, but still, the kite will allow me to observe the wind, the wind above the water.*

It will be as it was. For as long as she allows it, I will come to this house. I will come, and I will bring a gift and she will cook and we will lie together in her bed and she will bathe and smoke and I will watch and then I'll go home.

He opens the tobacco tin and reaches inside to straighten the dent that he made, sets it on the shelf. The woman rises from where she's sitting on the bed. She stands before the stove for as long as it takes for him to replace the blankets, the pillow at its head. Then she walks to the door and she opens it.

She holds it open until he gathers his things and leaves.

A LONG PUNISHMENT, but, he supposes, not longer than he deserves. Despite the fact that she won't open the door, neither to let him in nor to accept any conciliatory gift, Bigelow finds comfort in her presence—she's there, in her house. Every day he checks and sees that she hasn't left. On occasion, she even meets his gaze through the window. She looks at him, unblinking, for whole seconds before she turns away.

And the days grow longer; this alone makes him optimistic. En route to her house he feels the rush of birds overhead, returning, flying so close to the ground that their wing beats set the air shuddering around him.

It's just a matter of time before she takes him back. He cannot imagine any other outcome, and while he waits, he is building a new kite. He has what he needs—spars, muslin, wire, notebooks filled with calculations, his field book recording details of all but the last flight—and undertakes the project as a distraction. A copy, he thinks when he begins, an exact replica. He can reinvent what he lost.

But as he sits drawing at his table, Bigelow has a sudden, new idea. What if the cells were not square but triangular? What if, between two grand triangles . . . Bigelow starts with a fresh, unmarked page.

An hour passes, and another. Geese cry out, and when someone knocks he doesn't lift his head. Upstairs, a bird must have hit a windowpane. After all, visits to his station house are few.

Where was he? A central deck, between the two triangles, on which to mount equipment. If he increases the distance between the two cells, then—

"Hello?" A man's voice calls out. Another knock, louder.

Bigelow stands stiffly from his chair. He tucks his shirt into his trousers with ink-stained hands. When he opens his door, the man before him has already removed his hat.

"Davison," he says, and he holds out a hand. His shirtsleeve, just visible inside that of his coat, is fastened with a cuff link, and Bigelow, who doesn't care about such accessories, notices the gleaming stud, a thing he hasn't seen since his arrival in the north, not even on an undertaker. *Cuff link.* He says the words silently to himself, hearing their strangeness.

"Secretary to Mears. Engineering Commission." Davison looks past Bigelow into the station house, the drafting table with its piles of drawings. "You're the kite operator," he says.

Bigelow steps back from the doorway, inviting him inside. "I'm . . . I work for the Weather Bureau."

Davison nods. "You flew the kite. The box kite." With his hat, he gestures in the direction of the town. "They said this is where you live."

Gone, Bigelow is about to tell him, but instead he answers, "Yes."

"We need aerial photographs." Davison pulls out the one chair from where Bigelow tucked it under his table. He sits, leaning forward, an elbow on each knee. "We have the camera. Aluminum body. Weighs only four pounds. One exposure at a go. Then you have to reel it back in. Change the plate.

"What we need is this, we need survey photographs. Topographical, for the port. Deepwater port. There's five sites proposed, and we need to pick the right one. Need to see as much as we can. From above." Davison stands and walks once around the table, looking at the drawings. He picks one up, studies it, replaces it on top of the others. Then he looks at Bigelow. With his hands shoved in his pockets, he rocks back and forth on his heels.

"Commission's looking for an experienced operator. Someone who can fly a camera over the water. We had a fellow lined up, fellow with a biplane, but the wind's not right. He backed out." He shrugs. "The camera equipment's not complicated. Automatic shutter. But getting it into position—that's the trick. Timing device activates the shutter. Gives you as long as you need to get it where you want it. Hour. Half hour. You set it." Davison points out the door. "Photographs of the town, the creek, the inlet. All the environs."

"Environs." Bigelow repeats the word. A word like a cuff link, gleaming in his station house, calling attention to itself. He says nothing more, and the man, Davison, seems to interpret this as reluctance.

"Commission'll advance you more than enough to cover expenses," he offers, and as if he's already paid Bigelow for the privilege, he picks up the whole sheaf of drawings. But he doesn't look at them. His eyes are on Bigelow.

"How much?" Bigelow asks.

Davison replaces the drawings on the table. "Five hundred up front. Another fifteen hundred when we get the photographs. Satisfactory photographs," he adds.

Bigelow nods, mouth shut, determined not to betray any surprise.

"Two thousand total," Davison says, to emphasize. And Bigelow puts out his hand, the hand with the scars.

"When?" Davison asks, grasping the hand, not letting go. His palm is dry and hot. "How soon?"

Bigelow points at the table, his drawings. "I'm building a new kite. Better than the last one. Easier to control. Certainly at the altitudes you'd want for survey photographs. That's what, four, five thousand feet?"

Davison shrugs.

"But it will take—I don't know—a month. Two."

Davison lets him go. "June?"

"Maybe. The sewing's what's slow."

"Five hundred dollars," Davison says. "Up front." He puts his hand in his pocket as if about to produce the money. But then he leaves it there. "Hire someone," he says.

"Maybe."

"June?" Davison asks again, and Bigelow nods.

"I'll have an agreement drafted. You can stop in the commission office on Monday to sign. Take a look at the camera. Collect your advance."

From the station window, Bigelow watches Davison walk back toward town, his shadow so long it spills off the road. Then he puts on his coat and hurries after him, running where the man had walked.

At the woman's house he knocks at the door and then, when she doesn't answer, comes around to her window, cupping his hands to see past the reflection of his own face.

"Marry me," he calls to her, and she looks up from what she holds in her hands, her dress, dripping over the filled tin tub. Her braid, so black against the white of her underclothes.

"Marry me!" he says again, loud enough that anyone passing by could hear his words.

Bɪɢᴇʟᴏᴡ sᴘᴇɴᴅs ᴀ ᴅᴀʏ, and then another, at his desk, doing the math, pages of calculations to determine the advantages of an equilateral over a right triangle, and then, having settled on equilateral, pages more to decide the placement of the keel spar, the optimal distance between the two cells. He gives the ground floor of the station house over to the building of small-scale test models, for which he uses newsprint rather than fabric lifting surfaces, the entire room littered with bits of string and sticks and paper—paper everywhere, some pieces filled with notations, others snipped into shapes, stuck with glue to the surface of his table, his floor, the soles of his boots.

It's just a matter of time, he thinks, before she opens her door to his knock. Before she takes a gift from his hands and invites him inside.

Each afternoon, he makes a detour past her house. He stops and he knocks, he waits and he listens, he leaves a rabbit on the step and goes around to her window and peers through. Sometimes she looks at him; sometimes she doesn't.

But she accepts his gifts; or at least she doesn't leave them lying on the ground. She doesn't clean the marks left by his hands, his forehead, and even his mouth, from the spotless glass pane.

And on the day she sees a kite in his hands, a model ready to test on the bluff, she gets out of the chair. She comes closer to get a better look.

Bigelow steps back, away from the window. He lets a little of the line out, and the kite sails over his head. She watches, close enough now to press her cheek to the glass. Then she comes around to the door; he hears the latch as it gives.

The kite is ten yards out, flying over the street, and he offers her the line. He takes her hand and closes her fingers around it.

"This is nothing," he tells her.

She watches it with one eye closed against the glare. Bright enough on this spring afternoon that ice thaws underfoot. Minutes before, as he walked to her house, puddles were dull, gray, still slushy. Now they mirror the sky. The difference of one degree.

"Just wait until I take you with me," he says. "Up the bluff, with a real kite. A big one."

He stands behind her as she flies the model, reaches around to loosen her hold, let it out a few more feet.

When she lets him in, he sets the kite down, but it doesn't stay put. A draft blows in from under the door, and it slides along the planks with a whisper. Bigelow has to use a chair to trap it in the corner, far enough from the stove that he needn't worry. He can leave it and follow her to bed.

Unbutton his trousers and push up her skirt, anxious to be inside her, afraid of wasting even a minute on foreplay. Because what if she changes her mind?

JUNE 21. Solstice. The sun will never set on this warm day.

She lets him take her hand as they walk up the hill. Flowers break underfoot. He listens as their steps fall in and out of rhythm.

In a lifetime, only a handful of days like this one. The sky unfolds, and the wind cooperates. And the new kite—a hundred times prettier than the one he lost. Seams perfect, because she has sewn them.

He looks at her, standing by the shed, her face tipped up, loose strands blowing from her braid. She puts her hands up to shade her eyes.

With him she sees how it is: the leap into the heavens, the sun striking the white cells, the inlet's water spread like a glittering endless cape.

The kite scatters a flock of swallows, climbing.

What will he show her from a perspective of four or five thousand feet, from the vantage of the clouds?

A grid of houses, and hers among them. His station and his flags. The shed on the bluff, and next to it the reel. The bays of Cook Inlet. The scribbled path of the creek.

Three tattooed lines.

Two bodies in a bed.

A man walking track.

A rain of blue-and-white china.

The trumpet of a gramophone.

The wet black eye of a seal.

Cracks of light from between the warped boards.

God exhaling clouds of geese.

Copper siphon.

Column of mercury.

Each hour hanging like a pelt from her hands.

Taken together, one image laid over another, they will make a book of maps.

The outlines of a life.

ACKNOWLEDGMENTS

The author wishes to thank Gretchen Ernster, Joan Gould, Colin Harrison, Courtney Hodell, Jessica Kirshner, Kate Medina, Christopher Potter, Jennifer Prior, and Amanda Urban.

The equations on pages 133–34 are adapted from Lewis Fry Richardson's *Weather Prediction by Numerical Process,* published by Cambridge University Press in 1922. The box kite described in this work of fiction is inspired by those built by Lawrence Hargrave, whose late–nineteenth-century kite experiments in New South Wales, Australia, contributed much to aeronautical science.

In researching the early years of meteorology, the author is especially indebted to *Weather Forecasting in the United States,* published by the Weather Bureau in 1916; to those issues of the *Monthly Weather Review* published (also by the Weather Bureau) between 1913 and 1916; to Henry Helm Clayton's 1923 text, *World Weather;* to Donald R. Whitnah's *A History of the United States Weather Bureau;* and to Mark Monmonier's *Air Apparent.*

ABOUT THE TYPE

This book was set in Garamond, a typeface designed by the French printer Jean Jannon. It is styled after Garamond's original models. The face is dignified, and is light but without fragile lines. The italic is modeled after a font of Granjon, which was probably cut in the middle of the sixteenth century.